REPLAY

Also by Steven Sandor in the Lorimer Sports Stories series

Playing for Keeps

REPLAY

Steven Sandor

James Lorimer & Company Ltd., Publishers
Toronto

James Lorimer & Company Ltd., Publishers, acknowledges the support of the Ontario Arts Council. We acknowledge the financial support of the Government of Canada through the Canada Book Fund for our publishing activities. We acknowledge the support of the Canada Council for the Arts, which last year invested $24.3 million in writing and publishing throughout Canada. We acknowledge the Government of Ontario through the Ontario Media Development Corporation's Ontario Book Initiative.

The author makes a special thanks to the Ontario Arts Council's Writers' Reserve Program for research and development of the manuscript.

Cover Design: Tyler Cleroux

Library and Archives Canada Cataloguing in Publication

Sandor, Steven, 1971-
    Replay / Steven Sandor.

(Sports stories)
Issued also in electronic format.
ISBN 978-1-4594-0382-6 (bound).—ISBN 978-1-4594-0381-9 (pbk.)

    I. Title. II. Series: Sports stories (Toronto, Ont.)

PS8637.A547R46 2013   jC813'.6   C2012-908239-2

James Lorimer & Company Ltd.,
Publishers
317 Adelaide Street West, Suite 1002
Toronto, ON, Canada
M5V 1P9
www.lorimer.ca

Distributed in the United States by:
Orca Book Publishers
P.O. Box 468
Custer, WA USA
98240-0468

Printed and bound in Canada.
Manufactured by Friesens Corporation in Altona, Manitoba, Canada in February 2013.
Job #82158

For my most awesome wife, Noelle.
You are my anchor and my light.
And for Tate and Nico — our two little superstars.

CONTENTS

1 THE JADE GARDEN

Warren Chen lifted up the shiny, silver gate. The steam came hissing out of the machine. A tray of clean dishes, still hot, slid through the open gate.

It was seven o'clock. Warren had a half hour to empty the dishwasher and restock the dishes in the dining room. Then, with his homework already done, he'd be free to watch the game.

The Jade Garden sat on the lone main street of Sexsmith, Alberta. It could have been any of the hundreds of family-run Chinese restaurants in small towns across the prairies. The buffet table was filled with containers of food: crispy fried chicken balls and the bright red sweet-and-sour sauce that coated them, beef cubes in a yellow sauce, fried rice with shredded eggs. And for the customers who wanted a break from Chinese food, there were pizza slices and French fries.

Sam, the cook, hunched over the deep fryer at the other end of the kitchen.

"Dishes done, Warren?" he said. "Show me what you've got!"

Warren sped off to get a rolling cart. As he darted through the kitchen, he imagined he was on a football field, dodging tacklers. In his head he heard the voice of the TV commentator. "It's Warren Chen with the ball. He's broken a tackle! He's at the 30, the 20, the 10! Touchdown!" Warren zipped around Sam and dashed into the storage area where the carts were kept. He pushed the cart back to the dishwasher, skidding to a halt right in front of it.

Warren reached in, grabbed a dish and placed it on the cart. Then another, and another. His hands whooshed back and forth in a blur, like the movements of his favourite comic-book superhero. Soon there were four neat stacks of dishes on the cart.

Another tray came out of the dishwasher. Warren grabbed the containers filled with forks, knives, and spoons. He sorted them into a cutlery tray on the cart. He heaved the cart and it bolted forward through the swinging double doors that led out of the kitchen and into the dining room of the Jade Garden.

Warren had a glance up at one of the five flat-screen televisions on the walls of the restaurant. The pregame show was on. He still had time.

Warren sped forward past the red calendars by the kitchen doors, sliding underneath the gold dragon snaking across the ceiling, fangs showing, tongue hanging out. He took a quick corner around the host's table and its black porcelain lucky money cat, bulging eyes and a wide grin on its face, its battery-operated paw swinging round and round.

Warren swung the cart through an aisle. He swerved around his mother, who was serving a pot of tea to a family of four.

The plates wobbled and wobbled as Warren sped toward his goal — the buffet table in the middle of the restaurant. The stacks on the cart rocked back and forth, but the plates didn't come crashing down.

Warren's hands went into motion. The towers of dishes on the cart were slowly taken apart and then reassembled on the serving table. Warren grabbed handfuls of forks and put them in the cylindrical holders. He had to slow down a bit for the knives — he didn't want to cut himself. But the spoons clinked so quickly they sounded like he'd dropped them all over the floor.

Warren turned around to see if anyone noticed how quickly he had filled the table with plates, forks, knives, and spoons. But the diners were either lost in their own conversations or looking up at the TVs, waiting for the game to start.

Warren shrugged and sped with the cart back toward the kitchen. But just as he was ready to push through the swinging doors, a customer got up from a table and walked right into his path! Warren drove both of his heels into the carpet, braking the cart before he ran down the boy in his path.

It wasn't just anyone that Warren had almost run over. It was Brad Yellowdirt, the captain of Sexsmith's Grande Prairie Bantam League football team, the Shamrocks! Brad was almost six feet tall. His head was shaved, with just black stubble on his scalp.

"Brad! I'm s-s-s-s-orry," Warren stuttered. He couldn't believe that he was talking to the star quarterback — because he almost crashed into him with a food cart.

"No problem," smiled Brad. "I should have looked before I got up. Where's the fire?"

"I need to get done before the game," said Warren. "Calgary and Hamilton tonight."

"The Stampeders should win it easy," said Brad.

"I love football," Warren blurted out. "I've been to all the Shamrocks games. And I'm coming to tryouts next week . . ."

"Hey, that's great," Brad said. "The team can use every player it can get. Bring those quick feet and hands to the practice field!"

Warren charged through the kitchen doors. Brad Yellowdirt thought he could help the football team! Wow!

He skidded past Sam and pushed the cart back into the closet. He still had seven minutes to go before kick-off. Not his fastest run, but not bad!

2 CLOSE CALL

Warren burst out of the kitchen and sat in a booth in the back corner.

He looked up at the TV. The Stampeders in their bright-red home uniforms clashed with the Tiger-Cats in their white, black, and yellow jerseys. He settled in to watch the game.

It was a nailbiter. The game went to halftime tied 10–10. And four points separated the teams when they got to the fourth quarter. Except for a quick run to the kitchen to grab more plates at halftime, Warren didn't take his eyes off the screen. As the game clock wound down, Warren was joined at the table by his father.

"Time for my football lesson?" asked Warren's father as he sat down.

"That's right, Dad." Warren had lost count of the times he had tried to explain the game of football to his father. But that didn't mean he wasn't going to stop trying. Warren wanted his dad to understand why he thought it was the world's greatest sport.

Ever since Warren was a small boy, he'd loved the game. When most kids were watching cartoons, Warren was spending hours watching football and leafing through sports magazines.

"Son, I arrived in Canada almost twenty-five years ago from China, and I still don't understand this sport," said Warren's dad. "Having the games on the TVs is good for business. It keeps customers in the restaurant. But the game doesn't make any sense to me. It stops and starts and stops and starts. How do you follow what's going on? And why, after the whistle, do the players all gather in a circle?

"It's kind of like chess, except with players on the field instead of pieces on the board," Warren said. "The players gather in a huddle. It's so they can plan what's going to happen the next time the ball is snapped."

"Snapped?"

"That means when the ball is back in play. Then you can run, throw long, throw short — and there are lots of fakes. And that's what they talk about in the huddle. The quarterback tells his offence what they are going to do, and the players on defence try and guess what the other team is going to do. It's a strategy game as much as it is about running and tackling. You want to keep the other team guessing. Look, look! You see? Calgary threw the ball on that play, and the pass was knocked down by the Hamilton player. The Tiger-Cats — that's the Hamilton team — guessed that Calgary was going to throw the ball, and they were right."

"And you want to play this game? Why do you have to play it? You still want to try out for the Shamrocks?" Warren's dad sighed and shook his head.

"Yes, Dad." Warren had just celebrated his birthday and he was finally old enough to play for the Shamrocks. The team would be starting its fall camp the next day. The timing was so perfect, it's like it was meant to be.

"You're not big for your age, son. You know that. The players I see on TV, they are like monsters. This is a game for giants."

"I know it looks like that on TV, Dad. But not all the players at Bantam level are that big."

"But aren't *some* of the players that big? What about the players on the other teams?"

"They can't hurt me if they can't catch me!" Warren smiled at his dad to let him know everything would be all right. "I've gone to a bunch of Shamrocks games. It isn't like what you see on TV. These pros are the biggest and fastest players you will find anywhere. The Shamrocks and the other teams in the league, we are all just starting out. I will be fine, Dad. I know it."

"And you might not make the team," said his dad.

"That's not what I heard," said Warren. "The best player on the team told me they needed all the help they can get! Sexsmith isn't a big town, the coach needs more kids to try out — he doesn't have to make cuts!"

"Still, don't get your hopes up," said Warren's dad

before he got up from the table. "I know how much football means to you, but it's just a game."

Before he disappeared through the swinging kitchen doors, Warren's dad turned once again toward his son. "Remember our deal; you can try out, but you still need to keep up your marks. And I still need your help here in the restaurant."

Warren nodded and smiled at his dad before he refocused on the game on the screen. The Tiger-Cats had the ball late in the fourth quarter. But after the quarterback threw two incomplete passes, the Tiger-Cats had to punt the ball to the Calgary Stampeders. The Stamps would get one last chance to try to score a touchdown and win the game.

Warren's dad emerged from the kitchen, pushing a cart with steaming trays of noodles, rice, and colourful stews of vegetables and cubed meat. He stopped at his son's table.

"How much longer left in the game?"

"About two minutes, Dad," said Warren. "Hamilton didn't get the ten yards they needed to get a first down. Because they didn't get the ten yards, they will punt the ball to Calgary."

"Okay," laughed Warren's father. "I am not even going to try to pretend to understand that. How about a simpler question: Who is winning?"

"Hamilton, 20–16 over Calgary."

"Oh, close game?" Warren's dad said. "That's why I

heard so many cheers out here. You know that I need you to help wash dishes as soon as the game is over, right? But, first, Mom is going to bring dinner out for us."

As Warren's dad pushed the cart to the buffet, Warren's mom came to the table with Warren's younger sister, Lynn, trailing behind. His mom pushed another cart with four covered silver trays. Warren knew one tray held his favourite — ribs with black-bean sauce. The dish was delicious, but he knew his mom had to cook it in a corner of the restaurant kitchen. While it was being prepared, it gave off a strong smell, sort of like sweat socks.

Warren used to ask his dad why they didn't put the ribs on the menu.

"We don't want to offend the customers," Warren's dad would always say. "They want ginger beef. They want sweet and sour pork."

When Warren went with his family on a trip to Hong Kong, he found that no one there ate sweet and sour sauces or ginger beef. But they did eat black-bean ribs.

Once the buffet was restocked, Warren's dad joined his family at the table as Warren's mom set out the silver trays on the table.

"Why are you watching this stupid game?" Lynn asked her brother, who hadn't taken his eyes off the screen.

"Shh," said Warren.

Warren's dad turned his eyes up to the screen. There was a loud roar coming from the stadium.

"What's happening now?" Warren's dad asked his son.

"Forty seconds left. Okay, more like 35. Calgary is down four points. But if they score a touchdown for six points and kick the extra point, they'll be up three. They have the ball on the Hamilton 10-yard line. But if they don't put the ball in the end zone here, then Hamilton gets the ball and will run out the clock."

Warren's dad nodded, even though his glassy eyes showed he didn't understand a word of what was being said.

"This is stupid," whined Lynn.

Warren, like almost all the patrons in the restaurant, held his breath as the ball was snapped. The Stampeders quarterback dropped back to throw, but no one was open to catch the pass. The quarterback ducked under a defensive lineman who was looking to sack him. Before another Tiger-Cat could get to him, the desperate quarterback heaved the ball, hoping that it would fall in the arms of one of his teammates. A mass of Calgary and Hamilton players gathered in the back of the end zone, all leaping for the ball. Through the pack, one set of arms reached up and snatched it. Then the pile of players fell backward, a mass of bodies collapsing together. The referees rushed toward the play.

One by one, the players got up. The Stampeders put

their arms straight up, the universal signal that a touchdown has been scored. The Tiger-Cats crossed their arms and shook their heads, their way of saying "no touchdown."

Lying just behind the end zone was the Calgary receiver. The ball was in his arms. He got up, spiked the ball mightily and leaped up in the air. He pointed to the heavens. He ran to the head referee, putting up his arms.

The referee looked at the receiver, then put up his arms, too.

Touchdown!

"He caught it!" cried Warren. "Calgary's going to win . . . Oh, darn."

"Why do you say 'darn'?" asked his dad.

"Because both teams are stupid," said Lynn.

"Calgary is ahead of Edmonton in the standings," said Warren, ignoring his sister. "And the Stampeders beat the Eskimos last week," said Warren.

"And we like the Eskimos?" asked Warren's dad.

"Edmonton is closer to us," Warren said. "A few hours down the highway. Our team! And Calgary is Edmonton's biggest rival!"

"Hey, kid," cried Brad from a neighbouring table. "Not so fast. We have to see if the touchdown is good."

"The referee will look at an instant replay, to make sure that the player actually scored," explained Warren to his dad. "Basically, they will double-check their work. That receiver needed to have at least one foot in the field of play. And he couldn't be juggling the ball at the time he stepped out of bounds. He had to have the ball in his hands."

"I don't think it's going to count!" Brad yelled from his table.

Warren looked up at the screen. Various camera angles showed the Calgary receiver getting to the ball and bobbling it, and the whole pile of players falling backward.

But the mass of players falling out of the end zone hid the view of the receiver's feet. No matter what the camera angle, no shot clearly showed if the touchdown should count or not. The commentators explained that, if there was no replay that clearly showed if he was in bounds or not, the touchdown would count, as that's what the referees called on the field.

Meanwhile, the player who claimed the touchdown was running up and down the sideline. He was screaming, hollering. He pounded his chest. When he saw the sideline camera zoom in on him for a close-up, he pointed to his foot, then yelled "Touchdown!" loud enough for the audience watching the broadcast to hear.

After ten minutes of reviewing replays, the head referee went to the middle of the field and announced to the crowd through his microphone that the replays were "inconclusive." The touchdown would count.

And Warren and the restaurant patrons watched the Calgary players dancing in the middle of the field, celebrating a last-second win.

★★★

A photographer from the *Calgary Sun*, parked behind the end zone, had taken the shot that was used in papers across Canada and across the Internet after the game. Taken from directly behind, it clearly showed both the receiver's feet touching the white end stripe and the ball in the air — he was out of bounds and didn't have control of the ball. The touchdown should not have counted.

Warren was looking at the picture on an iPad the next morning.

"What's got your attention?" asked his dad.

"The game from last night. Turns out that winning touchdown shouldn't have counted."

"Oh, really? Why?"

"Because the player was bobbling the ball and fell out of bounds."

"So why did he celebrate like that?"

"To fool the refs, I guess."

"So he's embarrassed now that everybody knows, right?"

"No, no, no," Warren laughed and shook his head. "It says that his coach praised him for tricking the officials and getting his team the win. Here, read it for yourself."

Warren passed the tablet to his dad and started in on his breakfast.

"Warren, what kind of sport is this that you like?" asked his father. "What that player did is cheating. And everyone is acting like he did a great thing."

Warren pretended that he couldn't answer because his mouth was full. One look at the sadness on his dad's face, and he didn't know what to say.

3 A REAL WORKOUT

Warren stood on the sideline. The sleeves of the green practice shirt hung past his elbows. The shoulder pads looked like they were going to collapse on top of his small frame.

He recognized a few of the boys standing next to him. Some of them went to his school. Some came into the restaurant. But none of them were people he could call his friends. There were also boys from nearby small towns and hamlets, places with mysterious names like Spirit River and La Glace.

Then Warren felt a tap on the shoulder. It was Brad.

"Great that you came to try out," said the Shamrocks captain. "Well, it's more like practice. I don't think the coach is going to be cutting anyone."

Warren counted the players and saw there were just enough to have offensive and defensive teams. Still, he was too nervous to say anything.

"Did you see the news today?" Brad asked.

Warren responded with nothing but silence.

"That's funny," said Brad." I remember you explaining to your dad about that touchdown call. It's all over the papers, the Internet and TV today. And now you don't have an opinion?"

Warren worked up the strength to answer Brad. "I saw it. Front page of the sports section. The photo."

"Okay, good," Brad smiled. "I wanted to make sure you could still talk. If we are going to be teammates, we may as well get to know each other. You know, talk. Communicate."

Warren nodded nervously. "Do you think he *knew* he was out of bounds?"

"Of course he knew," said Brad. "But he did what any pro player would do. He sold the call. When the play is close like that, you convince the referee you're right, even when you know you're wrong."

A loud voice suddenly rang across the field. "Gentlemen, are you here to chat or are you here to work? Sprints, now!"

Coach Henderson was standing nearby, wearing a black and green Shamrocks sweater, a whistle hanging from his neck. He turned to Brad and Warren. "Hey, you two. Actually I am glad you are talking about last night's game. I'll say this, it was a shameful way to win. It's embarrassing when you are exposed as a cheat — and that's what's happened to that receiver. But enough of that! I need to see some sprints. Move!"

The field was located right behind the community

centre, across the train tracks from the main part of town. If you looked one way, you saw the chipped aquamarine paint of the old grain elevator that towered over the small town. If you looked the other way, it was all green fields and scrub brush. Coach Henderson had to yell to be heard over the noise of cricket chirps from the open meadows behind the football field.

Brad and Warren ran back onto the field. They lined up with about thirty other boys, all wearing green practice jerseys. They did a lap around the field, trying to ignore the biting mosquitoes.

After running, the boys were placed in two long lines for a drill. The boy at the front of each line ran five yards, then lay down. The next boy ran five yards past that point, then hit the grass. Then the next boy. This went on until everyone in the line was lying on the field. But the drill wasn't finished. The boy at the rear got up and ran to the front. Then the next. Then the next. From far away it looked like a giant green snake slithering through the field. But Warren found that it was exhausting. He had to pop up, run as hard as he could, then drop. With equipment on, it was like exercising on a hot summer's day wearing a winter coat.

After the boys had run three times each, Coach Henderson called for a break. He followed them to the sidelines as they went to gulp from their water bottles.

"Thanks for coming out this year, boys. As you know, there's room for all of you on the team. In fact, we could actually use a few more players, so if you have any friends who want to play, bring them out. But just because you made the team doesn't mean you can take it easy. I'll still cut any one of you who misses practices or isn't working hard. I'd rather have fewer players who are all committed to the cause than a lot of guys who just show up when they want to."

Coach Henderson called Brad and another quarterback over. He told the rest of the players to get into two lines. Warren was at the back of his line and couldn't see around the players ahead of him.

"Some of you here are new," said Coach Henderson. "No tackling yet for you. I need to see how you turn, how you catch the ball, how you run."

It was Warren's first drill as a Shamrock. He knew that, while the coach didn't have to cut players, it was still important to impress him. If Warren didn't do well, he could end up sitting on the bench.

The player at the front of the line would make a quick run into open space and then try to catch the short pass that one of the quarterbacks threw his way. The runner had to keep his feet moving as he caught the ball. It was the quarterback's job to hit the moving target.

Warren was in Brad's line. Each time a receiver was ready, Brad would call out, "Ready . . . ball!" The assistant coach would flip him a football. Then the first player in line would make his run.

The first pass was too far ahead of the receiver.

"Sorry, I'm a bit rusty!" Brad yelled.

The next ten passes all hit the receivers in the hands. Some made clean catches, some of them bobbled the ball, but none of them let the ball hit the deep grass.

It was Warren's turn.

"Ready . . . ball!" Brad cried.

Warren sprinted forward. As he looked at the quarterback, he saw the ball rocketing toward him. It was too high! He leaped as high as he could. The ball grazed his fingertips as it went by.

"Sorry, my bad," called Brad, pointing to himself.

"No, Warren should have caught that," said Rocky, the assistant coach. "We have a saying here: 'If you can touch it, you can catch it.'"

Warren felt his heart sink into his stomach. His heart sank all the way to his toes when he heard a voice from the line of players. "Can't blame the quarterback, the target is so small."

Coach Henderson blew his whistle.

"I heard that! Everyone, stop this instant!" he yelled.

The chatter stopped. All was quiet, except for the crickets.

"You are all here to support your teammates, not put them down," said the coach. "If I hear any of you making fun of a teammate like that, you will have so many laps around this field you'll be dizzy for a week!"

Warren heard a meek "Sorry" from the crowd of boys.

"Okay, then," Coach Henderson said. "Let's go."

And again they went, each boy running as hard as he could. The next time it was Warren's turn, Brad's pass hit him in the hands. Warren held on to the ball. The assistant coach clapped. Warren felt his nerves settle. *I can do this!* he thought.

Warren lined up and went again. Brad threw another perfect pass. Another catch. Then another.

Coach Henderson blew his whistle. He stood about ten yards in front of one line, while the assistant coach stood in front of the other.

"Here it is," said the coach. "Each of you will run up to me or Rocky, then do a hook. That means you turn as fast as you can and face the quarterback. The hook is all about timing. The quarterback will throw the ball before you actually turn around. When you do turn around, the ball will be right there, and you have to react fast to catch it.

"Oh," Coach Henderson added, smiling. "If the ball gets past you boys and hits either me or Rocky, you have to drop and give us five push-ups."

The first boy dashed out of the line and turned around just inches in front of Coach Henderson. The ball went through his hands and hit the coach in the shoulder.

The receiver dropped to the grass and strained through five push-ups.

By the time Warren got to the front of the line,

the field was littered with boys doing penalty push-ups. Brad called for the ball and Warren began his run, looking directly at the coach's stomach. He got as close as he could to Coach Henderson, then he spun. His fingers stung as the ball hit his hands. Brad had put some mustard on the pass, but Warren held on.

"Good!" yelled the coach.

After the passing drill was done, the coach gathered all the players to the middle of the field. They got into a circle around the coaches.

"Our first game is in three weeks against the Grande Prairie Raiders," said Coach Henderson. "If we are going to win football games, we need to be able to run as hard and tackle as tough in the fourth quarter as we do in the first. That means we have to build our stamina. Sure, we can all run fast for the first two or three plays of the game, but will you be able to give the Shamrocks all you've got on the fiftieth play of the game? We're going to find out!"

The players had to do jumping jacks, burpees, sit-ups, and push-ups. Coach Henderson called out which exercise they had to do, and they kept going until he told them to switch.

He blew a whistle, and the boys took a break. It seemed to Warren that they got to rest for about five seconds.

"Okay, that was the first quarter," said Coach Henderson. "Now, second quarter!"

The boys went through the exercises again, then the whistle blew.

"Okay, halftime!" yelled the coach. "Only two more quarters to go!"

Warren's arms shook under the strain of the push-ups. His stomach muscles burned as he struggled through more sit-ups than he'd ever done before. Warren felt aches in muscles he didn't even know existed.

Coach Henderson clapped his hands to urge on his players. "You need to make it through four quarters. You boys are watching too much TV. Look at you huffing and puffing! At this rate, you won't make it to half-time of our first game."

Warren got through the third quarter, then the fourth. Finally, it was over. Warren lay in the grass, trying to catch his breath. It was only Monday, and the two hours of practice were the hardest of his life. But he knew he'd be back on Wednesday, wanting more.

He finally got up, prying the green helmet off his head. He stumbled through the gate, following the other players in a line toward the dressing room. They walked past the sign that read "Where the Shamrocks Grow," with the picture of players silhouetted against a setting sun.

In the dressing room were pictures of all the previous teams. For luck, Warren sat under one of the team's two championship banners.

"You did okay out there," Brad said to him.

"Really?"

"Yeah. You'll be fine. Keep working hard."

"You don't think I'm too small to play?"

"We need everyone we can get," said Brad. "We lost to the Raiders by 40 points last season, and it still drives Coach Henderson nuts. They have a bigger pool of players to choose from. We just have to try to hold our own against them."

Brad didn't need to tell Warren about the game. Warren had watched it from the stands. Grande Prairie was up by three touchdowns at halftime. They had played most of their second-stringers in the second half — and still added to the lead.

As Warren unlocked his bike from the rack in front of the community centre, Coach Henderson stopped him.

"Look, Warren, I saw you out there. You made some nice catches. But, son, you are a lot smaller than the other boys, and younger too. I am not going to cut you. But I need to ask if you are sure about this. Is football for you?"

"You'll see, Coach," said Warren. "I can do this. I have wanted to do this for years. You need to let me try. Please."

"All right," said the coach. "No tackling for you yet. Team policy is that, in practice, you play with kids your own size. Frankly, no one on this team is your size. But you do seem to have a good set of hands. You haven't had to give me any push-ups yet. You're quick. We'll just have to figure out how to harness that."

4 SOMETHING TO PROVE

At the next practice, Coach Henderson divided the players into small groups. Brad and a few other kids were with a group of larger-than-average players. A few more were placed in a group of kids who were normal for their age — not too big, not too small, not too heavy. A group of really big kids were put in the pack of lineman. Some smaller kids were put together.

Coach Henderson had all the players put into their pods. All of them except for Warren.

"Coach, what about me?" Warren asked.

"I have a job just for you, Warren," said the coach. "You're going to be our kicker."

Kicker! Warren didn't want to be the kicker. It wasn't even like being on the football team! The kicker got on the field only a few times a game. He didn't tackle, he didn't catch the ball, he didn't run.

Coach Henderson clapped his hands and the boys all went off to work in smaller groups. The coach found a spot in front of the goalposts, placed the ball on a tee and turned to Warren.

"Don't worry, son. At least this way you'll get to play," said the coach. "Let's see what you can do."

When Warren was younger, he used to run into the schoolyard at recess and cut through imaginary blockers. He would dash in and out, seeing himself racing down the sideline toward the end zone. At no time did he see himself kicking off or trying to hoof extra points and field goals.

But what was he to do? Say no?

So he sighed, took a mighty run toward the ball and tried to put his right foot through it.

The ball went off the side of his foot and travelled about four yards to the right before coming to a rest.

Embarrassed, Warren strolled over to the ball. He picked it up and put it back in place. Coach Henderson held it again.

This time the ball went to the left about six yards.

And so it went. Five kicks. Ten kicks. Twenty. And not one of them got close to going through the uprights.

"Just keep working on it, Warren," said Coach Henderson. "That first game against Grande Prairie is in a few weeks. We'll get this right."

Warren knew that there was probably someone else on the team who could kick instead of him. Didn't the Shamrocks have a pretty good kicker?

But if Coach Henderson wanted him to kick, what

choice did Warren have? Would he have to carry water bottles? Or worse, be cut? Not being on the team was an idea Warren wasn't willing to consider.

For the next week, Warren showed up to practice and went right to the kicking tee. As he tried in vain to put the ball through the uprights, he could hear the other players running and tackling. He heard them laughing and shouting words of encouragement. He heard Brad, the team leader, telling the receivers how to run their patterns.

Warren had never felt so alone. He was thankful every practice when it was finally time for the exercise sessions.

After a practice that seemed to last forever, Warren got on his bike. As usual, he rode downtown. He ducked through the back alley and in through the back door of the restaurant. He was greeted by a blast of hot air from the kitchen. He waved to Sam, who was about to drop a basket of breaded chicken into the deep fryer.

Warren dashed to the rack where the white aprons were hung. He quickly draped one across his hips, picked up a bussing tray and headed into the dining room. He stopped at a table and started to place the dirty dishes and cups in the tray.

"What time is it, son?" Warren heard his father's voice.

"Oh, hi, Dad." Warren turned to see his father standing behind him, his arms folded.

"You promised you would be back here by six." His father took a long, pointed look at his watch. "It's almost six-thirty."

"Well, practice ran late . . ."

"Warren, you said you'd be here at six. If you make a promise to someone, you have to keep it. I'm not concerned because practice went long. I am concerned that you made me a promise you didn't keep."

Warren knew that when his dad was unhappy, he didn't yell. He simply talked calmly, but forcefully.

"And Warren," his father went on, "did you have a chance to get to your homework before you got here?"

"I just have a bit of math homework to do tonight," Warren answered. "I will catch up after I've cleared the tables."

"Just a *bit* of homework? One day, you put off a bit of homework. Next day, you put off some more. Next day, you have a mountain of work that you haven't caught up on. You can't make this a habit."

"Yes, sir."

Warren's father pointed to a table that had yet to be cleared. It was filled with half-full tea cups and plates smeared with sauces.

"Now, finish clearing this one table and put the dishes in the dishwasher. Then leave it to your mom and me to do the rest. Get that homework finished. You can help later."

What Warren couldn't tell his father was that he

wanted to bus and help serve the tables. That's because it was Wednesday. Each and every Wednesday, the Mason family came to the Jade Garden for dinner. And if Warren could help fill their water glasses, maybe — just maybe — Bridget Mason would talk to him. Or smile at him.

Warren felt a little shaky whenever Bridget came into the restaurant. This queasy feeling had begun a few months ago, and he couldn't explain it.

At school, he didn't dare go near her. After all, why would she want to talk to him? He was the scrawniest kid in the class, not nearly as tall as Bridget. What girl wants to talk to a boy who's smaller than she is?

But at the restaurant, maybe she'd thank him for filling her water glass or for bringing her a clean bowl. The problem was, he couldn't do those things if he was stuck in the corner of the Jade Garden finishing his math homework.

Warren went back to clearing the table — as slowly as possible. He put the plates in the tub one by one, gingerly placing them one on top of the other. The more time he took, the more chance he'd see the Masons . . .

. . . walk into the restaurant! The front door opened and there they were, Bridget in the lead, a silver-coloured camera hanging from her neck.

Warren went from lingering over the dishes to speedily sliding them into the tray. He dashed as quickly as he could to the kitchen, where he stacked the dishes on the conveyor belt that led into the maw of the dishwasher.

Warren pushed through the door to the dining room, grabbing a pitcher of ice water from the serving area. He went to the Masons' table and filled the water glasses.

"Thank you," said Bridget's mother.

Bridget aimed her camera at the gold dragon that snaked its way across the wall over their heads. She twisted a dial and then took a shot. Then another twist of a dial and another shot. This time, a flash went off. Then she carefully focused and took another shot without the flash. Warren knew that Bridget was president of the school photography club, but he had never seen her take pictures before.

"How long have you had that dragon?" Bridget asked Warren, not looking away from the golden form on the wall.

"As long as I can remember," Warren said.

"Its eyes sparkle from the way they catch the light," she said.

Warren felt his dad's eyes on him.

"Sorry, have to go," he said and walked away. Bridget had talked to him!

Warren's dad was at the serving table as Warren returned the pitcher.

"Homework. Now," he said.

Warren walked toward the family table in the back

corner of the restaurant. His backpack was sitting on one of his chairs. His dad had retrieved it from the kitchen where Warren had dropped it, so it was ready and waiting for his son.

Warren unzipped the pack, pulled out his math textbook and a workbook, then sat down. He was surprised when his father sat down across the table from him.

"Warren, I know you want to help me here in the restaurant *and* do your best in school, too. That's why I worry that playing football makes it too much for one boy to handle."

Warren looked up from his textbook. "Dad, I've wanted to play football, to be on the Shamrocks, ever since grade school. I want to prove myself." He thought about the practices filled with endless kicking. "Well, I wanted to prove myself, but . . ."

"But?"

Warren gritted his teeth. "Being on the team isn't what I thought it would be like. I'm going to be the kicker. That is, if I can even do that right. That's all I do. Kick. All I'm proving is that Coach Henderson thinks he has to protect me from really playing." Warren hoped his father didn't see the tear running down his son's cheek. "And that's why I was late," he said. "Kicking after practice. Just to see if I could get that right."

"But you stuck with it?" asked Warren's dad. "You kept kicking because that's what your coach wanted?"

"Yes," Warren replied quietly.

"Son, that's not something to be embarrassed about. You took on a job; you didn't walk away. That's a good thing. You know there are no such things as small jobs. Most people who own restaurants started off as busboys."

Warren got up from the table and walked as fast as he could into the kitchen, away from the customers. The only thing worse than crying in front of his dad would be if Bridget Mason spotted the small kid weeping in the corner of the restaurant.

5 FIRE IN THE BELLY

Warren's right foot was sore from kicking the ball, again and again. The opening game against Grande Prairie was coming up fast.

Every practice, Coach Henderson would offer words of encouragement.

"You'll get this."

"Warren, just be patient, it'll come."

"You can do it."

That was the weird thing, Warren thought — it was called *foot*ball, but there was really very little kicking to be done.

One practice, after the players had done their burpees, sit-ups, push-ups, and jumping jacks in the circle, Coach Henderson blew his whistle. Practice was over . . . or so they thought.

Brad didn't remove any of his gear. He jogged over to Coach Henderson.

Coach Henderson blew his whistle again and Brad bellowed, "Guys! Gather up! Everyone. Don't go to the dressing room yet."

As the number-one quarterback, Brad was the leader. If he said practice wasn't over, his teammates wouldn't leave the field, even if the low sun would make the ball look like a dim spot lofted into a darkening sky. The team formed a circle around Brad and the coach. Warren couldn't actually see over the other boys to look at Brad — but he could hear his quarterback's voice.

"Look, we still have a few minutes. We have a big game against Grande Prairie coming up. I know we are tired. And we need to work. So let's divide up into teams. Half the guys on this side, half the guys over there."

Warren stood up, ready to head back to the kicking tee.

Coach Henderson put up his hand. "Wait, Warren. Please go on Brad's team. No more kicking for you today."

No kicking! Warren was so excited he slammed the helmet back down over his head hard enough to feel a rush of air flood into his ears.

"Okay, Brad's team is going to take the kickoff," said the coach. "Warren is going to return the ball. I have heard he's the world's fastest busboy. Let's see if it translates to the field!"

Warren couldn't believe it. He stood twenty-five yards from the end zone, waiting for the kickoff. A line of players stood in front of him. The ball was kicked and sailed end over end through the air. The Shamrock who kicked the ball was one of the team's slotbacks. His kick went much farther than anything Warren could have kicked.

Warren was off like a shot, as fast as his legs would take him — one, two, three, four, five, six steps to the left. And there the ball was, in his hands.

"Go!" yelled Brad.

"Go!" yelled Coach Henderson.

Warren saw a stream of defenders coming toward him. He ducked under the first tackler. He was still on his feet. A hop and a skip to the right, then a fake left. And then he dashed to the right, beyond the outstretched arms of two more would-be tacklers.

Another defender came, but he tried to hit Warren high up on his body. Warren simply ducked underneath. He kept going.

Thirty yards to the end zone.

Twenty.

Warren hurdled over the hands of another would-be tackler.

Fifteen yards. Ten. Five.

Warren crossed the goal line and collapsed. Touchdown.

Coach Henderson tossed a clipboard into the air. "Wooo-hoo!" he yelled.

"Fluke!" cried one of the tacklers Warren had evaded.

Warren rose from the ground, arms in the air. "Then let's do it again!"

"You sure?" said Brad.

"Yeah!"

The boys lined up again. This time the kicker hit the ball low and it bounced wildly several times before Warren could pick it up.

But Warren got his hands on it. The group of tacklers waiting in a circle around him converged as soon as Warren touched the ball. Warren suddenly realized that being small wasn't so bad. Being so low to the ground made him hard to knock over. He bounced off a couple of tacklers but wouldn't go down.

He emerged from the scrum, then jetted down the left sideline. Touchdown. Again.

Warren spiked the ball in the end zone and turned to look back at his Shamrocks teammates. They were all huffing and puffing after their vain attempts to bring him down.

Brad started to clap. And then the coach. And then another teammate. And another. Warren stood and let the wonderful sound wash over him as the sun set.

After practice, before Warren could head into the dressing room, Coach Henderson stopped him.

"Warren, you showed me something: that you have a big heart. And a lot of courage. You came here practice after practice and kicked and kicked. I wanted to see how dedicated you were to playing football, and you proved you'd do anything to be a Shamrock. You are still the smallest player on the squad and just barely old enough to play. I probably won't put you on the field a lot, but I won't make you kick. You passed my test."

Test? Warren was stunned. He looked at Coach Henderson, wide-eyed. "But I thought the team needed a kicker . . ."

Coach Henderson smiled sheepishly. "Pete Garrett is one of the best receivers in the Bantam league. He also kicks and punts. He's coming back from an exchange program in time for the GP game. So I thought I'd challenge you. Warren, you met that challenge. You worked hard at kicking, and today you worked hard at carrying the ball. You were impossible to stop. You have the heart to play this game."

"So you never wanted me to be a kicker?" Warren asked slowly.

"Warren, you will always have trouble convincing people you can play because of your size. So you need to have a fire in your belly. And if I just let you have a position, it wasn't going to light that fire. I wanted to see you fight for it. You did."

The coach's words still echoed in his ears as Warren got on his bike. His bike flew over the railway tracks. He zipped down Main Street. All he wanted to do was burst into the restaurant and tell his dad the news.

Warren sprinted into the Jade Garden. His dad was in the office, going through the books with his mom.

"Mom, Dad!" Warren was panting but was still able to blurt out, "Coach said I don't have to kick! I can play! I can PLAY!"

"What does that mean?" asked Warren's mom.

"What it means," said his dad, "is that your son stuck with something and that he impressed his coach."

Warren's sister walked over from the family table.

"You're going to play that stupid game?" she asked.

"Now, now, Lynn," said Warren's dad. "You don't understand the game. I don't understand the game. But it's not stupid to work hard to achieve a goal you've set for yourself. Warren did that. We'll all talk more about it — after Warren has finished his homework."

But Warren had already walked over to the family table and pulled a history textbook from his backpack.

6 ON THE BENCH

Warren had felt the butterflies building in his gut from the moment he woke up that morning. With each passing minute they got worse, as if his stomach was shaking him from the inside.

His mom had made his favourite breakfast: chicken with oatmeal. He could barely touch it.

"Today is your big game," she scolded. "Eat!"

But all Warren could do was sip tea and watch his food get cold. His father read the newspaper across the table.

"Dad?" Warren asked.

"Yes?" His dad's face peered out from behind the business section.

"Are you coming to the game today? Kickoff is at noon. It's only a five-minute walk from the restaurant."

Warren wasn't sure if he wanted his dad to see the game or not. He wanted his dad to see him run down the field with the ball tucked under his arm, dodging tacklers. But he also wondered if seeing his dad in the stands would make him more nervous.

"Saturday afternoons are busy at the restaurant, you know that. A lot of people coming in for lunch. Big day for families. And I am already down a busboy."

Warren knew *he* was the busboy in question.

"You told me you won't play very much, if at all," Warren's dad continued. "Isn't that what the coach said?"

"But it's Grande Prairie," Warren said. "This is the team we want to beat the most. In the Grande Prairie paper, they predicted they would beat us by forty points."

"So you want me to come to see your team lose by forty points?" His dad raised the newspaper above his eyes, almost hiding the hint of a smile on his face

Warren was surprised to find that the giant weight pressing against his stomach and lungs was lifted. Warren could handle being nervous about the game if he didn't have to worry that he would disappoint his dad. He grabbed a spoon and downed a hearty scoop of chicken and oatmeal.

After breakfast, Warren hitched a trailer to his bike. His parents used to tow Lynn around town in it, but now it held Warren's football bag and helmet. He rode off and turned down Main Street, past a large poster in a shop window that read: "*Bantam Football Opener. This is the year the Shamrocks beat Grande Prairie!*"

As he rode down Main Street, Warren saw Brad,

teetering on a bike laden with equipment. They both stopped.

"Nervous?" asked Brad.

"Should I be?" replied Warren.

"Last year we got killed. These guys are monsters!"

"But we worked so hard this week," Warren said. "And didn't coach tell us that if we worked hard, anything is possible?"

"*Possible* is different from *probable*," said Brad. "We practised hard last year, too. And we got crushed. Warren, Grande Prairie is thirty times the size of Sexsmith. They actually have tryouts and cut players. Heck, they can recruit the best players in the area. And here we are, having to take anyone we can get."

Warren looked down at the sidewalk. He felt like he was going to throw up all over his shoes.

Brad stuttered, "Oh, uh, s-s-sorry, Warren, I didn't mean . . . I mean —"

"No, Brad," Warren interrupted. "You're right. Our team has to take anyone. That means anyone like me. I wouldn't be big enough or strong enough to make the Grande Prairie team."

"But Warren, you should see yourself in practice," said Brad. "You're quick. You can move sideways and forward and this way and that. Fast and agile can be as good as big and strong."

Warren didn't answer. He began pedalling again, and Brad followed. The rest of their ride was over all too quickly. When they got to the community centre parking lot, they saw Grande Prairie Raiders arriving in their parents' cars and vans. The players were huge. They didn't look like boys who were just entering their teens.

The Shamrocks gathered in their dressing room, every member of the team quiet. Not a word was spoken.

Coach Henderson walked in.

"What's going on here?" his voice boomed. He was wearing a Sexsmith sweatshirt and his whistle, as always, hung from his neck. "What is this? A funeral? Boys, come on . . . this is football! We've been preparing for this game for weeks!"

A couple of the boys clapped half-heartedly.

"Coach, I saw them out there," said one of the Shamrocks. "They're huge. Their smallest player is as big as our biggest player."

A couple of the boys nodded.

"So you're scared, huh?" Coach Henderson paced through the dressing room. "When I was young, I was scared too. Not scared of getting hurt. But scared of looking bad. Boys, you control whether you look bad. Win or lose, you can hold your head high if you give everything you've got."

"You boys know that size isn't everything in football," the coach continued. "You need to be quicker. We need to be smarter. They can't tackle who they can't catch!"

"That's right!" cried Brad, looking around at his teammates.

"And you know what?" Coach Henderson continued. "You can play hard, maybe even hard enough to win. But don't do it for me. Don't do it for the town. Do it for your teammates. Gentlemen, I want you to look at the player sitting to your right."

Warren looked at Brad. And Warren felt the eyes of Dan Arcand, a lineman, on him.

"Now, I want you to make a promise to that teammate," Coach Henderson said. "Promise him that you won't let him down. That's the person you don't want to disappoint. That teammate. When you're on this team, wearing this uniform, we're family, we work together."

The applause came again. But this time, every boy on the team clapped. And the sound of the clapping grew louder and louder.

Brad got up and led the team through the dressing-room door, out into the hallway, past the equipment room, then out into the blazing sunshine. A green line of Shamrocks strode onto the field, their colours brighter than the grass. The Raiders, all dressed in black, were already on the field.

When the Sexsmith players got to the sidelines, Brad called them together. They gathered in a circle, each boy reaching a hand into the middle. Warren had to squeeze between a couple of linemen so he could get his hand in.

Brad spoke. "Remember what coach said. We are family. We hold our heads high. And let's win this game, for us!"

The boys in the circle whooped the loudest whoop they had ever whooped. Warren didn't feel sick to his stomach anymore. He felt like he was floating on air.

But after the stands had filled and the game had kicked off, Warren didn't feel like he was floating anymore. He felt like he was sitting on a cold, hard bench. Because that's exactly what he was doing.

"You'll get your chance, Warren, I promise," said Coach Henderson, as twelve Sexsmith players bounded out onto the field. "Just hang in there."

Warren, his coach and the other Sexsmith players on the sidelines could hear the chatter from the Grande Prairie players.

"Forty points again!"

"Maybe we'll let you score a touchdown . . . not!"

"Who are we going to send crying home to Mommy first?"

Warren watched Pete Garrett kick off. He knew he could never kick the ball that way, even if he practised for a hundred years. And he was glad he didn't have to try. The Grande Prairie returner settled under the pigskin. He caught the ball and began running up the field.

Over the last week of practice before the game, Coach Henderson kept telling Warren that he needed to protect the ball. He had to put two hands on it so that he wouldn't fumble if he got hit. Warren noticed the Raiders return man wasn't doing that. He was holding the ball in one arm off to the side.

So when the Raiders returner got hit, the ball popped in the air.

"FUMBLE!" Warren yelled from the bench.

"*FUMBLE!*" Coach Henderson yelled from the sideline.

A pile of black-shirted Raiders and green-shirted Shamrocks players piled on the bobbling, loose ball. One by one, they were peeled off the pile by the referees. Finally, at the bottom was a Shamrock, the ball cradled in his arms.

The Shamrocks on the sideline leaped into the air. The crowd roared. "The ball is ours!" cried Warren.

The fumble shocked the Raiders. Within a minute, Brad threw for one touchdown. He ran in for another a few minutes later.

The crowd, except for the visiting families of the Raiders, were on their feet, clapping and chanting. And then Warren saw her — Bridget Mason — walking behind one of the end zones, a green camera bag slung over her shoulder. Warren hoped she wouldn't take a picture of him sitting on the bench.

With each play, Warren looked hopefully at Coach Henderson. He willed the coach to tap his shoulder and tell him he was going in. But he just sat.

Even from his seat across the field, Warren could

hear Grande Prairie's coach screaming at his players. *I bet even people in Grande Prairie can hear him*, Warren thought. The Raiders coach was shouting at his players to take their opponent seriously, to stop being so cocky; to get down to work.

The yelling worked. Despite being down 14–0 early in the game, the Raiders roared back after their coach's tirade. Warren felt helpless as the Raiders defence stopped the Shamrocks offence on play after play. And when the Raiders had the ball, they smashed forward. As the clock moved toward halftime, the Shamrocks' lead had been trimmed to just three, the score 20–17.

When just a few seconds were left in the half, Warren got up and walked to his coach's side.

Warren didn't need to say a word. Coach Henderson knew why he'd come to him.

"Warren, I will try to get you in. But remember, these are the biggest players in the league. By a lot. And I have to protect you."

The referee blew his whistle and waved his red flag in the air, the signal for halftime.

The Sexsmith players ringed Coach Henderson. Warren was one of the few not reeking of sweat and sucking in huge gulps of air.

"Boys, we have done something that hasn't been done in a decade," Coach Henderson said, waving his arms. "We are up on Grande Prairie!"

"Yeah!" cried Brad, pumping his fist.

"Coach," one of Sexsmith's linemen uttered between gasps, "we're not gonna hold on. They're bigger than us. They're so much faster."

The Raiders were roaring back early in the second half. After taking the kickoff, the Sexsmith team had the ball. A running play saw them gain zero yards. And Brad was sacked 10 yards behind the line of scrimmage. Sexsmith punted away, and the Raiders came down the field. After five minutes of punishing runs, Grande Prairie scored another touchdown. After the extra point, it was 24–20 for the visitors.

Sexsmith was forced to punt once again, and the Raiders got a field goal. The score was 27–20.

7 THE
RETURN

Since taking an early 14–0 lead, the Sexsmith Shamrocks had been outscored by the Grande Prairie Raiders 27–6. It didn't look good for them heading into the fourth quarter.

As the Shamrocks players couldn't move the ball, the only offence the team could muster came off the foot of Pete Garrett. He unleashed an amazingly long punt that bounded into the Raiders end zone. It got Sexsmith a single point, making the score 27–21 for Grande Prairie.

Coach Henderson pleaded with his defence, knowing the Shamrocks could not let the Raiders score again. If the Raiders extended their lead to more than a touchdown, there wasn't enough time on the clock for the Shamrocks to make a comeback. As long as the Shamrocks stayed within a touchdown, there was hope. On one play — a long passing play from Brad to one of his receivers, a big interception or a fumble return by the defence — the team could get into the end zone and take the lead.

"Just stay tough! Don't let them make plays!" Coach Henderson pleaded with his defensive unit as they huddled on the sideline.

That's when Warren started to notice how much those exercises at the end of every practice had paid off. The Grande Prairie players were getting tired! After each play, their hands were on their knees. They weren't able to make big runs on the Sexsmith defence anymore.

For what seemed to Warren like an awfully long time, Grande Prairie would take the ball and have to punt. Then Sexsmith would take the ball and have to punt. Back and forth it went, like a game of ping pong. There was one small ray of hope. Pete hit a second booming punt that rolled into Grande Prairie's end zone for a single point. That made the score 27–22.

Warren could hear the sport commentary in his head. *"This stalemate is good for the Raiders. They have the lead. They aren't going to win by 40 points like last year, but they are going to win."* Each time the Raiders defence stopped Brad and his offensive team, the visitors got closer to victory. Time was the enemy of the Shamrocks.

Warren looked toward his coach, and Coach Henderson met his gaze. *I can make a play,* thought Warren. *Put me in.*

There was less than a minute left to play in the game. Then thirty seconds. Warren stared at his feet, hanging over the bench. His cleats were still shiny and black, with no mud or grass on them. He sighed.

Warren knew that if the Raiders got a first down, they would be able to run the final few ticks off the clock. The game would end and the win would go to the Raiders. But if the Shamrocks could stop them, the Raiders would have to punt. That would give the home team a few seconds to try for a big return, to try to snatch the win from their rivals.

The Raiders quarterback dropped back and tried to make a quick pass to the running back. But Sexsmith's tacklers were quick. Two Shamrocks combined to knock down the running back right after he'd caught the ball, far from the first-down marker.

Coach Henderson called a timeout. There were only fifteen seconds left, time for just one more play. He tapped Warren on the shoulder.

"We have to take the punt and hope for a miracle," he said. "Warren, it's your turn now. Show me what you showed me in practice."

Warren couldn't help but notice the Grande Prairie players pointing at him as he ran onto the field.

"Really?" he heard one Raider player yell. "Him? I thought he was their mascot!"

"He's smaller than the ball!" He heard another Raider laugh.

The ball was snapped back to the Raiders punter, who lobbed the ball into the air and then swung his right foot through it. The ball wobbled end-over-end in the air. Warren saw that it was going to land in front of him. When the short, bouncing punt landed, it spun on one end and then popped awkwardly up above the grass.

After waiting nearly four quarters for his chance to play, Warren was ready. He'd been waiting for this chance since he arrived at his first Shamrocks practice. He got his legs moving, broke forward, and snatched the ball out of the air.

Warren spun. He had just a moment to react. No tackler could be within five yards of the punt returner when he first touched the ball. It gave Warren time to make a step to his left, then another. He saw a wave of black jerseys coming toward him. So he reversed direction.

The end zone was seventy yards away. Warren ran away from the pack of tacklers and cut up the field as he got toward the right sideline. His feet skidded on the grass as he turned. He was just inches from going out of bounds. He looked like someone learning how to skate, except he was wearing cleats and sliding on the grass instead of on ice.

Warren got his balance. He tiptoed as he turned so he wouldn't go out of bounds. Then he put his head down and ran. He saw a black-and-silver Raiders tackler coming from the side. The Raider dove at Warren's feet. Warren leaped in the air and over the sliding Raider. Warren landed, stumbled, and then resumed his run.

He was forty yards from the end zone.

He looked to see what other tacklers could be coming from his left. But they were fading in the distance.

Warren was thirty yards from the end zone.

Through the roar of the crowd and hollers from his teammates on the sideline, Warren couldn't hear anyone coming from behind. But he had a feeling that he still had one tackler to beat. He looked quickly over his shoulder. There was a black shirt coming right from behind, gaining on him.

Warren was twenty yards from the end zone.

He put his head down and pushed forward, even though his lungs felt as if they were on fire.

Warren was ten yards from the end zone.

Five yards.

Three yards.

Warren felt the arms of his pursuer wrap around his ankles. Warren's legs went out from underneath him. Desperately he thrust his upper body forward and reached the ball toward the goal line. All he had to do was to get the point of the ball across the front of the line — that's all he needed for a touchdown.

Warren hit the ground . . . and saw that the ball was about a half-yard short of the goal line.

As quickly as it had come, his chance to be a hero was snuffed out.

Or was it? Warren's mind raced as he thought about the games he'd seen on TV, how the pros danced and showboated after they scored. If that Calgary player had fooled the officials and won his team the game, couldn't Warren do the same?

Warren freed himself from his tackler and spiked the ball in the end zone. He reached his arms up in triumph. The crowd cheered.

The referee ran to catch up to the play. He looked at the tackler, who kept slashing his arms back and forth, mimicking a *No Touchdown* call. The Raiders came running over the sideline stripe and onto the field, to congratulate their defender for making the game-saving tackle. Coach Henderson and the rest of the Shamrocks ran onto the field to celebrate the winning touchdown.

There were two sets of players on the field, both celebrating. But no player on either team was as animated as Warren. He rolled on the ground, kicking out his legs. The referee looked at Warren, who screamed, "Yeeaaahhhhhhhhhhhhhh!"

But the referee had yet to make his call. There was no instant-replay booth. It was up to the head referee to make up his mind, based on what he had seen.

And the longer the referee waited to make the call, the louder Warren became. He knew there was no going back. Once he had started yelling and screaming, he couldn't quit. He looked at the Grande Prairie tackler, who was also cheering loudly. Warren thought that if he yelled louder than the Raider defender, if he jumped higher than the Raider defender, then maybe that would help the referee make up his mind.

And then the referee put both arms up in the air, signalling a touchdown.

At that moment, the mass of Shamrocks players descended on Warren. A sea of green engulfed him.

Warren reached his hand through the pile of players, raising a finger in the air.

8 CELEBRATION

Warren was on the goal line, lying underneath a mass of green-shirted teammates. Dozens of guys — all much bigger than Warren — had piled on to celebrate the winning touchdown. Really, it should have hurt . . . a lot. But the adrenaline rush had pushed Warren to the point where he didn't feel pain.

As he heard the players screaming through the earholes of his helmet, Warren realized he was feeling something other than elation. It was a weird feeling in the pit of his stomach, like being hungry but needing to throw up at the same time.

Finally, the players picked themselves up one by one, until only Brad and Warren were left on the ground.

"That was sick!" Brad yelled. "That was maybe the greatest football play I have ever seen! Not in an NFL game. Not in a CFL game. In a Shamrocks game, right in front of my eyes!"

Brad stood up and offered Warren his hand. Brad pulled Warren to his feet and beckoned the Sexsmith players to come back on the field.

That's when Warren saw one Raider who refused to leave the field — his tackler. The Raider still had his helmet on, but Warren could see his eyes. They were glaring at him. It was if the defender was trying to stare right through him.

And then the defender pointed at Warren. One long, accusing finger. And Warren's feelings of being hungry and sick to his stomach at the same time got even stronger.

But then his stomach lurched, as he was hoisted up into the air and settled onto a precarious perch on the shoulders of his teammates. They moved forward en masse, holding Warren high. They headed toward the bleachers, which were filled with screaming fans. The parents of Raiders players quietly stared at Warren.

The Raiders coach was on the field, yelling at the referee. The coach marched down to the one-yard line and pointed to the spot he thought Warren went down. The referee simply shook his head.

Warren was carried to the sidelines where he exchanged hugs with his teammates. Coach Henderson tapped him on the shoulder. "Okay, superstar," said the coach. "Time to address the masses."

Warren spun and looked at his coach, who was soaked in sports drink from head to toe.

"The masses?" Warren asked.

"Yeah, the press."

Behind the coach stood a woman in blue jeans and a denim shirt. She held out a smartphone that could record conversations.

"I'm Stacey Lynes from the *Herald-Tribune*," she said. "You're Warren? The kid who scored the touchdown?"

"Y-y-yes," Warren said. Right. He did score the touchdown. That's what the referee decided.

"That was such a close play to end the game," she said. "What were you thinking as you ran down the field?"

When Warren watched the highlights of NFL and CFL games on TV, the replays were shown in slow motion. They made it look like the players had a lot of time to decide what to do. But Warren had learned that, when he was on the field, everything happened so fast there wasn't any time to think.

"I don't know, it happened so fast. I mean, well, I was thinking about how much my lungs were burning. I was hoping I wouldn't fall. I looked over my shoulder and saw the other player coming up from behind me. I just put my head down and ran."

"About that tackle. I just heard Coach Klimchuk over on the Grande Prairie side. It's clear from how he is reacting that he thinks you didn't get in the end zone. I could hear him yelling that a few of his players on the field *swore* you didn't get in."

Warren felt the blood drain from his face. The feelings in his stomach started up again. Was somebody sure that he was short of the goal line? Did anyone in the stands see?

"Well, um, I was running for the line. I was in. I scored. The ref agreed."

"So you're saying you are 100 per cent sure the ball crossed the goal line before you hit the ground?"

"Yes," said Warren.

"Excuse me," said a voice from behind Warren. *Whew*, Warren thought, *someone is saving me from this grilling*. Then he recognized the voice.

Warren spun around and found himself looking up at his father.

"Warren, you did very well today," Warren's dad said, smiling. "Well, the people in the stands next to me said you did well. I saw you on the bench for most of the game, then you had the ball and it looked like the whole world was chasing you. Now they tell me you're a hero."

Warren blinked hard. "Dad, you're here."

"Of course I am here. I knew the big game was today. Heck, that's all everyone in the restaurant has been talking about for the last week. And I know how hard you have worked. You wanted this so badly. Besides," Warren's dad added, "the restaurant was empty. Most of the customers were here watching the game!"

The reporter cleared her throat. Warren's dad turned so he could look her in the eye. "Thanks. My son is done answering questions tonight."

The reporter sighed and walked away.

"What was she asking you about?" Warren's dad asked.

"She wanted to know if I really got into the end zone. She says the other team thinks I didn't score."

"That's a serious accusation. But you are too honest to do something like that. "

Warren's felt his heart plunge into his stomach. His father assumed that Warren was too honest to cheat, but that's what he had done. And now he had to hide it from his dad. His father being ashamed of him would be the worst thing ever.

"I have another question," Warren's dad said.

Oh, no, thought Warren. *What now? Is he going to want to know more about the touchdown?*

"Why is your coach all wet?"

"Oh," Warren said, relieved. "In football, to celebrate a big win, the team takes the big jug of sports drink and pours it on the coach at the end of the game."

Warren's dad scratched his head. "The more you tell me about this game, the stranger it sounds. The coach is okay with that? Really? I mean, that's a waste of sports drink. Isn't that stuff expensive?"

Warren shook his head and smiled. His dad didn't suspect anything. As usual, he was thinking about practical matters.

Warren's dad put his arm around his son's shoulders. The pads made Warren look twice his normal width.

"Now, go in, get changed, and meet me at the car."

"Okay, Dad. It's Saturday, and I know there will be lots of work to do at the restaurant tonight."

"Well, if you want to call eating your favourite meal 'work.' Mom made ribs with black bean sauce especially for you."

"What?"

"Win or lose, we planned a celebration for you. Son, we all know how badly you wanted to play football. I am proud you did it. We are all proud."

Warren couldn't believe how good it felt to hear his dad say he was proud of him. He tried to force out of his mind the image of the ball coming down short of the goal line. Maybe if he thought hard enough, he could convince himself that the point of the ball was across the front edge of the goal line. *That's it,* Warren thought. *The ball was across the goal line. Just by a smidgen.*

But he knew it wasn't. Not even close.

9 KEEPING A SECRET

Monday morning was cool and crisp. The town was still a month away from the first snowfall, but there were already yellow and brown leaves on the ground.

Warren skidded to a stop at the bike rack in front of his school and climbed off his bike.

As soon as he began to wrap the lock strap around the frame of his bike, he could feel the eyes on him. A crowd of students had gathered around.

There were cheers. He felt slaps on his back.

"What a finish!"

"The whole town is talking about you!"

"Greatest play in history!"

Warren was stunned. He felt a tingle each time someone congratulated him.

Wow, even the girls are talking to me, thought Warren. Usually, the only time girls from school ever talked to him was at the restaurant — and only for another serving of ginger beef or refills of soda. He wondered if Bridget Mason was waiting for the chance to speak with him.

Warren walked into the school and down the hallway to his locker. There were sticky notes posted on his locker door. They were covered with words like "Wow!" "Congrats!" and "Superstar!" Some were in rounded handwriting that gave away that they were written by girls.

Warren looked around the hallway at the eyes on him. Nobody asked him about whether or not he'd scored. All they wanted to do was shake his hand and talk about his punt return.

What am I worried about? Warren wondered. *Nobody here knows.*

Warren didn't pay much attention in math, English or his social science class. He stared out the window, thinking over and over about the people who were treating him like a hero. He thought about how his dad had told his mom and sister how proud he was of Warren during their victory dinner.

He thought about that Raider defender pointing at him. Warren blinked hard and erased the image from his mind. He knew if he thought about it too much, the weird feelings in his stomach would start again. Instead he imagined what he looked like, bolting along the sideline as Grande Prairie players tried to chase him down from behind.

Warren didn't take a single note that day. His pencil never touched paper, but he felt like it was the best day of school ever.

The only thing that could have made it better would have been getting a sticky note from Bridget Mason, or the chance to talk to her. He saw her across the hallway during class change, and he could have sworn she had looked straight at him and frowned.

After school, Warren biked through the historic downtown district, past the restaurant, across the tracks and to the community centre. The football team was crammed into the Shamrocks dressing room.

Coach Henderson's job was teaching social sciences to the high-school kids. Warren thought he looked just like a teacher, standing behind a digital projector hooked up to a laptop.

"In today's team meeting we'll go over our last game," he said.

Brad nudged Warren and whispered, "See? We got the biggest win ever, and this is where Coach Henderson's going to tell us everything we did wrong."

Warren felt the blood drain from his face. If Coach Henderson had a video of the game, would the phantom touchdown be revealed to the whole team? He felt his stomach start to churn again. And he realized how silly he had been to start believing that his secret was safe.

"How did Coach Henderson get a video of the game?" Warren asked Brad.

"He gets one of the parents to take a camera and shoot all the plays. Now Coach will show us the video to teach us what we did right and what we did wrong. Just like the pros."

Coach Henderson pushed a button on the projector and one of Grande Prairie's touchdowns was shown on the white wall of the dressing room. Coach Henderson told the safety he should have stayed in the middle of the field, rather than try to help a teammate cover a wide receiver by the sideline. He told the linebackers that they were slow after the ball was snapped.

"Hey, superstar," Brad whispered at Warren. "Why are you looking so nervous? It's not like the coach has anything bad to say about you. You got on the field and made the one big play."

"Um, Brad, I think I have something I need to tell you," Warren whispered back.

"What's wrong? You look like you're going to be sick."

"BOYS!" Coach Henderson's voice boomed across the room. His finger pointed at Warren and Brad. "We do this so we can learn from our mistakes. Just because we got one big play doesn't mean we played a perfect game. So please keep your conversation until after the video session. Respect your teammates!"

Warren swallowed hard.

"Even Warren has to pay attention to what I am trying to teach you guys!" Coach Henderson turned his attention to the rest of the team. "And that's what this is. It's a classroom. You are learning about football.

About teamwork. About depending on each other."

The video screen went dark. The room was quiet.

"Okay," sighed the coach. "It's not all about me telling you what you did wrong. Here's something that you did right."

Warren looked up to watch the play he had replayed so many times in his mind over the last couple of days.

On the screen of the dressing-room wall, he was scrambling to pick up the ball.

Oh no, he thought. *What if the whole team sees me fall short? Coach Henderson must have seen this already . . .*

Warren wished with all his might for a power blackout. Or was there a way he could get to the projector cord and yank it out of the outlet?

"This is a great job from Sam, Corey, and Avery here," said the coach as he pushed the clicker and the frame froze. The image? Warren running behind three blockers. "You created a nice wedge around Warren, allowing him to get a flying start. You created a lane for him. Good."

And then the video was in motion again. Warren watched himself turn up the sideline, then he exhaled. It felt like a giant weight lifted off his shoulders — the person with the camera didn't have a good angle. As Warren dashed down the field, the person with the camera had to follow the play from behind. So when Warren was brought down by the defender, the view was from the back. There was no way to tell where the goal line was.

A roar went up from the team as the Warren on the video got up and spiked the ball mightily.

Warren exhaled deeply. His secret was still safe.

Brad smiled. "So, Warren, what was it that you wanted to tell me?"

Warren looked away. "Oh, nothing. Nothing really. Let's just pay attention to Coach Henderson."

★★★

Warren retrieved the paper bag containing his lunch, and was just about to shut his locker door. He had planned to find a nice spot just outside the school to enjoy his noodles and some late September sunshine.

But his plans were interrupted by a tap on his shoulder.

He turned around.

Bridget Mason!

"H-h-h-ello," Warren stuttered.

She just said, "Warren. Come with me."

"Um, I was just going to eat my lunch," Warren replied, fighting the urge to jump in the air with joy.

"It can wait."

Bridget started walking down the hallway. She turned back and asked Warren, "Are you coming, or what?"

Warren stuffed his lunch back in his locker and closed the door. He followed Bridget down the hall.

What did she want? Everyone else wanted to talk to him about the touchdown. Why was she being so serious?

They wove through the crowded hallways until they got to the computer lab. It was empty.

"I'm with the photography club," Bridget explained. "I have permission to be here during lunch."

"Yeah, well, anyway, I'd been wanting to talk to you —" Warren started.

Bridget put her finger to her lips. "Save it. I have to show you something, and we don't have much time."

She sat in front of one of the computers. The screen flickered to life. Bridget fished a flash drive out of her jeans pocket and plugged it into a port on the back of the monitor.

Warren's stomach began to hurt. A lot. It was as if someone had just punched him in the gut. Or — since he'd never been punched in the gut — he felt how he imagined getting punched in the gut would feel.

Bridget had been taking photos during the game.

She pushed a few keys and said, "I had a chance to go through the pictures I took for the photography club. I have one to show you."

Bridget clicked the mouse and a picture appeared on the screen. There was Warren, reaching with the football toward the end zone. The Raiders tackler had his arms around Warren's legs. Warren's knees were clearly on the ground, and the photo showed a half-yard of green between the forward point of the football and the goal line.

"Did you know you didn't really score?" she asked.

"Um, uh, um . . ." Warren stammered. Someone had proof that he had cheated. And worse, it was Bridget Mason!

"I see," she said. "You *did* know."

"I just . . ."

"Well?"

"Bridget, have you shown this to anyone?"

"No. But I have to show some of my work at my photography club meeting."

"Any picture but that one!" Warren's tone became pleading. "Look, I'll do anything if you erase that pic."

"Anything?" Bridget's eyebrow shot up.

"Yes, please. If this gets out, I'll be humiliated."

"And everyone will know you are a cheat. And a liar, right? Because it's not like you *thought* you might have been in the end zone. Your reaction tells me that you knew you were short."

Warren didn't say a word. Here was Bridget Mason, the most beautiful girl in all of Sexsmith, and she had just called him a liar and a cheat. The worst thing was that she was right! Congratulations from every other person in the school didn't make up for how he felt right now. Warren tried not to look at Bridget or the computer screen. He just looked at his shoes. He looked at how they were worn near the toes, how the brown laces had become frayed at the ends.

"Well, Warren, you *can* do something for me," Bridget finally said.

She dragged the photo into the trash icon on the screen. "I'm erasing this flash drive. And I can erase the photo from the camera's memory card. Look, what I want is simple. I hear you're at the top of your math class. I don't do so well at math and my parents are really on me about it. I need you to help me. As in, help do my assignments. Or do them *for* me."

"What?" Warren said. "But that would be cheating!"

Bridget cleared her throat. "And that bothers you how?"

Warren looked at the way Bridget's eyes went wide when she cleared her throat. Just for a second, Bridget Mason wasn't the prettiest girl in Sexsmith anymore. But Warren closed his eyes and opened them again — and Bridget's face had returned to normal.

Warren thought about the trouble he could get into if someone found out that he helped Bridget cheat on her assignments. But then he thought about the picture of him being short of the goal line running in the sports pages of the *Herald-Tribune*. He thought about what people at the restaurant would say to his dad if Warren was exposed as a cheat. Helping Bridget wouldn't be that wrong, would it? Especially if they didn't get caught?

Warren nodded. "Deal."

"Okay," said Bridget. "You have me handled. But remember, I wasn't the only person there with a camera. The local paper was there. There were parents who were taking pictures and movies. My picture shows you didn't get into the end zone. It really wasn't close. So someone else might have proof, too."

"Oh." Warren thought again about a picture of him being tackled short of the goal line running in the newspaper. His heart sank.

10 A BAD EXAMPLE

Warren parked himself at the family table in the corner and hit the books. Within two minutes of his arrival at the Jade Garden, his pencil was already scratching across his workbook as he went through math problem after math problem.

It was Thursday night and the sooner he got done, the faster he could watch the football game on TV — Edmonton in Montreal. Because of the time difference between Alberta and Quebec, the game would kick off at 5:30 p.m. Alberta time. It barely gave time for Warren to finish school, attend the Shamrocks team meeting and get to the restaurant. And this time, it was going to be especially tough to finish before the game started. Not only did he have his own work to finish, but Bridget had handed him two pages of her math homework to do as well.

As soon as Warren finished the last of his equations, he reached into his backpack and pulled out Bridget's homework. According to their deal, he'd write out the answers on a separate piece of paper and she'd copy them onto the homework sheet before handing it in at school. The work had to be in her handwriting or they'd both get busted.

Bridget had also told Warren to get the answers to two questions wrong. She was struggling in math, so it would look suspicious if she handed in a perfectly correct paper. For now, getting 80 per cent correct would be good enough. As their plan went on, she'd get better and better results — to make her progression from D student to A student seem natural.

As Warren began to jot down the first few answers on Bridget's assignment sheet, he thought about how much planning she'd put into this. She'd instructed him to make her look good, but not *too* good. He had to not only do the homework, but also follow her instructions.

Warren got to a question she'd instructed him to get wrong. To Warren, it wasn't that hard — a fairly basic multiplication problem. Even though it wasn't his assignment to hand in, he found it hard to write *56* as the answer, rather than *63*. Warren was so deep into Bridget's homework that he didn't immediately notice when his dad sat down next to him.

"Oh. Hi, Dad," Warren said. He quickly put his arms over the paper in front of him.

"Good to see you hitting the books," Warren's dad said. "But why the secrecy?"

Warren mumbled something about making sure his

answers were right before showing anyone. Warren's dad waited for Warren to show him the piece of paper hidden under his folded arms. The stalemate was broken when Sam stopped at the table.

"Sorry, Mr. Chen," said Sam. "I need a hand for a second."

As his dad followed Sam to the buffet, Warren took the paper off the table and stuffed it back into his knapsack.

Warren's dad returned to the table just as the TV screens showed the Edmonton Eskimos and the Montreal Alouettes walking onto the field for the game-opening coin toss.

"Okay, explain this game to me again. I'll sit here and watch it with you. If you're so gung-ho to get your homework done in record time to watch, and if I am going to come and watch you play for the Shamrocks, I need to figure this thing out."

Warren poured tea for his father from the pot on the table into a small round cup. He then looked up at the screen, pausing to see where the ball was on the field. After he'd soaked up the information, he once again tried to explain to his father what was going on.

"Okay," said Warren. "Edmonton's in white, and they have the ball. They have two downs to get ten yards, or they have to punt on third down. Or, if they are close to getting a first down, then the coach can use third down to go for it rather . . ."

"What are downs? What's a punt?" His dad put his hands up in surrender. "Enough. I'll just try to follow the game and ask questions as we go along. You always say this is like chess. I tell you, chess is much easier."

Father and son watched the Edmonton quarterback loft the ball down the field. A Montreal defender collided with the Edmonton wide receiver as the ball arrived. The ball bounced left and right as it hit the turf.

"See, Dad," said Warren. "The ball isn't round, so you don't know how it's going to bounce."

"That's physics, not football," laughed his dad.

There were groans from the patrons in the restaurant who were watching the game dressed in green Edmonton jerseys and gold-coloured Edmonton caps.

On the TV, they watched as the Edmonton receiver bounced up off the ground and went to chase down a nearby official.

"Isn't he supposed to go back to where they all squeeze together?" Warren's dad asked.

"That's the huddle, Dad. That player is mad the referee didn't throw a flag for a penalty, so he's gone to argue," explained Warren.

The receiver yelled at the referee. He reached into his back pocket and threw an imaginary penalty flag onto the ground.

"He's just trying to embarrass the referee in front of everybody," said Warren's dad.

"Yeah," Warren clapped. "He's showing up the ref.

He's letting everyone watching know that the flag should have been thrown."

Warren's dad took his eyes off the screen and looked at his son.

"Why are you clapping, Warren? Do you think that's okay?"

"Sure, football players do it all the time."

Warren's dad sighed deeply. "Don't they ever just put their heads down, stay quiet, and get on with it? I certainly hope that player gets thrown out of the game."

"Why?" cried Warren. "He's just doing what players do all the time."

"I don't care who does what how much of the time. That's a disgrace. To him and his teammates. His coach should be embarrassed. So what if the referee doesn't call a penalty? Go back and make the catch the next time. Don't yell and scream and act like baby in front of thousands of people. People should laugh at him, not clap for him. Celebrating doing well is one thing, but arguing and play acting shouldn't be a part of the game."

For as long as Warren had watched football, he'd seen the pro players act this way. They danced after they scored touchdowns and argued with referees when calls didn't go the way they wanted them to go. It was part of the game. But why did he feel so uneasy about it when he watched it with his dad?

"Warren, promise me one thing," his father said as

he folded his arms and sighed. "Don't ever pull a stunt like that in one of your games. If I ever see you argue with a referee and jump up and down like that, you won't be playing football again."

Warren looked down at the table. He couldn't meet his dad's eyes. What would happen if his dad found out that his touchdown dance wasn't a true celebration, but the kind of play acting he hated?

11 MANNING MAULING

Coach Henderson tossed his clipboard on the ground as the crowd behind him cheered.

The Manning Royals had just scored their third touchdown of the game, their wide receiver dancing into the end zone after a Shamrock missed a tackle at the ten-yard line. The Royals just needed to kick the extra point to take a commanding 21–0 lead before the halftime break.

Coach Henderson ranted on the sidelines of Manning's community field. "This is what I was afraid of! We get the big win last week and what happens? We get lazy!"

The Shamrocks on the sideline kept their eyes forward, looking toward the field in silence. No player wanted to make eye contact with Coach Henderson. No player wanted to be pointed out — because it meant the coach might make him the scapegoat for a bad afternoon. He might remind that player of the blocks he missed or the ball he dropped. And on a day that saw the Shamrocks trailing by three touchdowns, it would be hard to find a player who hadn't made a mistake. It was best not to look up or say a word.

Coach Henderson picked up the clipboard and sighed. "Just a few seconds before halftime. We may as well hope for a big play on this kickoff return. Warren, get in there."

Warren felt his teammates slap him on the back as he crossed the sidelines onto the field. He also heard Manning's coach yelling from the other side of the field.

"Okay, let's do it again! Stop this guy. He may be small, but he's as slippery as a waterbug! Don't let him beat you!"

Wow, Warren thought. *I've got a reputation.*

But Warren didn't have long to dwell on how well-known he was in the town of Manning. The kick was off, the ball travelling end-over-end in the air. Warren settled under it and caught it clean. He saw that none of Manning's players were charging at him. This was going to be the last action of the half, and the Royals players knew that if Warren was brought down, Sexsmith would not have time to run another play. If the Royals could keep Warren out of the end zone, Sexsmith would have no more chances to score before the halftime whistle.

So they could allow Warren to gain fifteen, twenty or even thirty yards. It was better to all hang back than to have players charge up, miss tackles, and offer Warren a gap he could skip through to make the really big play.

Warren danced left, danced right. None of the Manning players shifted with him. They were waiting for him to make the first move. So he did, dashing all the way to his left toward the sideline. The Manning tacklers shifted, creating a wall of players that would not let Warren cut back to the middle of the field.

Warren charged forward, realizing that he would need to dodge a bunch of tacklers by the sideline. A Manning defender lunged at his legs. Warren was able to leap over the tackler.

But as he landed, he saw that his left shoe grazed the out-of-bounds line. He knew that even one end of a shoelace touching the line would end the play.

Warren wasn't sure if he heard the whistle or not. Just like in the game against Grande Prairie, things began to go in slow motion. He wondered if he should stop or keep going.

At that instant, he remembered what his dad said about the game they'd watched together. If he kept going, wouldn't he be cheating again?

So with his next step, Warren turned left and took a step outside the sideline. This time he heard the whistle. The head referee pulled a flag out of his pocket and waved it in the air to signal that the half was over.

Warren was running to where his team was gathered when Brad pulled him aside.

"What was that?" Brad asked.

"What was what?"

"You just stepped out of bounds and gave up on the play!"

"No," Warren shook his head. "I was already out of bounds. I knew the play was over and just took another step out."

"Play to the whistle!" hissed Brad before walking away.

Warren thought about following Brad and telling him what had really happened in the last game. He didn't want the team captain doubting his desire to do anything to help Sexsmith win.

Warren looked to where his dad was sitting in the stands. He had driven Warren an hour north up the Mackenzie Highway to get to the game in Manning. Warren suddenly didn't feel like telling Brad the truth about the Grande Prairie game anymore. They were in another game and were playing poorly. What difference would telling him make? He had to prove himself by what he did from that point.

"You guys are second best out there!" Coach Henderson roared at his team. "You are slow. You are taking it easy, taking your opponents for granted! Defenders, be ruthless. Offensive line, please give your quarterback some time to throw! Receivers, you have to be sharper!"

As the boys walked away, Coach Henderson told Warren to stay behind.

Uh-oh, Warren thought. *Is Coach going to tear a strip off me?*

Before that could happen, Warren blurted out, "Sorry, Coach. I stepped out because I was already out of bounds . . ."

Coach Henderson put up his hands. "Save it, Warren. That's not what I wanted to talk to you about. You had no chance on that play, anyway. The defence waited for you to make the first move, and you made a mistake. You ran to the sidelines, making it easy for them to corner you. You ran yourself into a spot where your blockers couldn't help you. Next time, when they hang back, stay in the middle of the field. Make them come to you. Eventually they will come."

"Oh," said Warren. "I thought it was about me going out of bounds. Kinda like last week . . ." Warren quickly shut his mouth.

"Huh?" The coach took off his baseball cap and scratched his head.

"Sorry, Coach. Never mind!" Warren power-walked away from the coach.

★★★

Coach Henderson is right: you really are only as good as your last game, Warren thought as he collapsed. He had just finished a set of lung-busting jumping jacks that closed the team's first practice after the loss to Manning.

The practice had been tough. Extra drills. Extra exercises. The receivers ran more patterns. At one point

Brad told the assistant coach he felt like his arm was going to come off, because he'd thrown pass after pass without a break.

By the time Warren got back to the restaurant, he ached all over. When he loaded the dishwasher, each plate felt like it weighed a ton. After his dad had locked up the restaurant for the night, Warren was too tired to catch the sports highlights on TV. He didn't remember falling asleep.

The next day, Warren was cleaning tables at the restaurant when a family called him over to their table.

"See, that's the kid. The touchdown hero," said the father to the mother.

"Pleased to meet you," the mom nodded.

The two children at the table waved. One of them, a girl about six or seven, waved a paper napkin at Warren. "Can I have your autograph?" she asked.

Don't these people know we lost our last game? Badly? Warren asked himself.

But all through the dinner service, he was stopped by customer after customer who wanted to talk about the touchdown from the game against Grande Prairie. The people of Sexsmith were still talking about the Shamrocks as if the Manning game had never happened.

Grande Prairie was a nearby big city, and the Raiders lost that game in Warren's home town. The loss to the Royals had been on the road, an hour away up the highway — and there was no rivalry between the towns of Manning and Sexsmith. Warren soon realized that the Shamrocks could lose all the games on the schedule — and they'd still be heroes for beating the big, bad Raiders.

But Coach Henderson didn't have those stars in his eyes. On Thursday, he again ordered the receivers to run patterns over and over. The linemen hit the tackling dummies again and again. That Saturday, it was the Peace River Prospectors who would be making the trip to Sexsmith to take on the Shamrocks.

"You guys found out last week what happens when you get cocky," said the coach in the dressing room after practice. "Don't ever believe you're the best at what you do — you always have to work harder, even if you're winning. You guys beat the Raiders and didn't think anyone could touch you. We won't make that mistake again!"

The coach pointed to the plaque on the wall that read "*Shamrocks, League Champions, 2000.*" Names were inscribed on it — the names of the players on the championship team.

"That team never took an opponent lightly. When you play the game, you respect the game. And that means always taking your opponent seriously. You guys thought Manning would be easy after we beat the Raiders on the last play of the game. We got what we deserved in Manning, gentlemen."

There was silence after the coach had spoken. After a whole week of gruelling practices, the Shamrocks felt like they were being punished. But Brad, Warren, and their teammates knew that their coach was 100 per cent correct. They had been too busy listening to the town telling them how awesome they were to practise as hard or keep working on improving themselves.

Brad finally got up and, as captain, spoke on behalf of the team.

"Coach, we won't let you down again."

12 CONSPIRACY

After a long Friday's worth of classes that felt like they would never end, Warren walked to his locker. He found Bridget waiting for him there.

"Don't worry," Warren said. "I have it. In the locker. I got question 15 wrong for you. The rest should be good."

"The homework can wait," she said to Warren. "We need to talk."

Warren again followed her toward the room used by the photography club, weaving through the halls, avoiding students and teachers. Bridget was power walking, moving so fast she was almost running.

"What is this about, Bridget?" asked Warren when they were finally in the room.

"Warren," she said, her voice quivering. "I think I messed up."

"What do you mean? Did you get caught with that last math assignment? Did your teacher figure it out?"

"No, no," she sighed.

"Then what?" Warren was getting worried. "Do you still have the photo?"

"I erased those photos from the memory card like I said I would."

"Okay, good." Warren nodded. "So what's the problem? Why are you acting so strange?"

"Because I realize I did something wrong. When I opened the photos for you, I dragged them onto the computer. That computer is on a network that runs through the entire school. And even though I erased them off the memory card, I am pretty sure I left them on the school server. That means any teacher, anyone who comes across the folder can see the photos."

Warren felt the blood drain from his face. "You mean that the photos that show me not scoring the touchdown aren't all gone?"

"No," Bridget shook her head.

"Well, erase them!" Warren said, trying to suppress the panic in his voice.

"I will, first chance I get. But I'll need time alone at a computer that's hooked up to the server to make sure I get it out of the system. I have to search and make sure there aren't copies anywhere. And, well, of course, it's wrong, too."

"Wrong?" Warren raised his voice. Then he realized that if he kept yelling someone would come into the classroom. He said in a panicked whisper, "It was wrong when we decided to make our deal. It's wrong for me to do your homework for you. But it's too late to go back."

Warren felt dizzy. He tried to think, to fight the urge to run out of the classroom, down the hallway and out of the school. Just keep running.

"Please, just do it," he said. "You've got to keep helping me. Please."

"Okay," said Bridget. "When I can get a few minutes alone on a computer, I will erase the photos of the touchdown. No one will know. I can't do it now. The hallway out there is too crowded."

As they glanced at the door to the classroom, they realized someone was standing at the door. The door that Warren hadn't fully closed when they entered the room.

Warren stared at the figure in doorway. It was Brad.

"I heard someone yell," Brad said. "What's this about?"

"Nothing," Warren said.

"Does this have something to do with how weird you've been acting?" asked Brad. "What's this about 'erasing the photos'?"

Brad looked at Bridget. "Do you have photos of Warren's touchdown? Awesome! Why would you want them erased? I should go tell Coach Henderson. He'll want to get one framed and put it up in the Shamrocks dressing room!"

"No!" Warren said.

"Why not?" asked Brad. "Seriously, at practice I'll tell the coach that she, she, she . . ."

"My name is Bridget," Bridget said.

"Yeah, right, Bridget. I will tell Coach Henderson that Bridget has a photo of the big touchdown!"

"Please, don't!" Warren had tears in his eyes. "Stop asking for them!"

"Why?" said Brad. "It's one of the biggest moments in Shamrocks history!"

Warren took a deep breath. There was no way out. Unless he told Brad the truth, Brad would tell the coach the photos existed — maybe before Bridget had the chance to erase them. He whispered, "Brad, the reason you can't have the photos is because there was no touchdown. I didn't get into the end zone."

"You didn't get in the end zone?"

"No." Warren wanted to dig a hole in the floor and then drop through it. "I wasn't in. I was short."

"Wow. I mean, WOW. So all that celebrating? Did you ever sell that call! Like in that Calgary game. Boy, Warren, I didn't think you had that in you!"

Warren nodded. "Well, I did. But, Brad, do you think what I did was wrong?"

Brad shrugged. "I don't know. I think we're supposed to do whatever we can to help the team win. That's what you did."

"Excuse me," Bridget broke in. "As captain of the Shamrocks, are you saying you are okay with this?

You're not going to tell your coach that Warren didn't get in?"

"No, I don't think I'll tell the coach," said Brad slowly. "As for the photos, I don't know about them. I never heard about them. Look, Warren, that was the biggest win for our team in years. It was the biggest win I've ever had. It wasn't just you. It's all of us — every guy on the team is getting the hero's treatment because we beat Grande Prairie. And I don't want that to stop."

"So we all agree to keep our mouths shut about this, right?" said Bridget.

Warren looked from Brad's face to Bridget's. "And we make sure those photos get erased for good."

★★★

Warren and his teammates were warming up in front of their parents and the fans. Kickoff was only minutes away and the Peace River Prospectors were on the other half of the field, gathered in a circle, jumping up and down and chanting.

Warren sat down and stretched, pointing his toes and trying to touch them while seated on the grass. Brad broke from a huddle, where he was talking to the wide receivers, and ran over to Warren.

"Warren, can I ask you something?"

"What is it?" Warren said, rising from the ground.

"It wasn't wrong to win that Grande Prairie game, was it?"

"Hey, yesterday you were the one saying that it was fine."

"Yeah, but I didn't sleep well last night. Actually, I didn't sleep at all. Felt like I wanted to run out the door and tell the world that I knew you weren't in the end zone."

Warren sighed in relief. Up until now, he felt all alone in covering up the lie.

"You too? Ever since that game, every time I think about what I did, I get this really strange, queasy feeling. I can't explain it. I've never felt anything like it before."

"Guilt," said Brad. "That's what it is. The guilt. I guess it's affecting us both. And we are both going to have to learn to live with it."

Warren and Brad jogged to the sidelines as the teams prepared for kickoff.

Coach Henderson pulled Brad aside.

"You okay, son?" asked the coach.

"Sure," said Brad. "Why do you ask, Coach?"

"Your throws in warm-up were all over the place. You sure you're all right?" "Coach, I'm fine," Brad said.

Warren was sent out to take the opening kickoff. He managed to slide by a couple of tacklers. He dashed for forty yards before he was brought down on the Prospectors half of the field. His teammates applauded as he returned to the bench.

"Good run, Warren!"

"Attaboy!"

"Nice one!"

Brad and the offensive team broke their huddle and lined up on the ball.

The ball was snapped. Brad took three steps back and fired a short pass up the middle. At least, that's what it looked like he wanted to do. The ball hit the ground five yards away from the receiver.

Coach Henderson grabbed at the bill of his cap and sighed.

On the next play, Brad dropped back to throw. He tossed it down the middle. There was not one, but two defenders who were covering the slotback. It was like Brad didn't see the defenders. One of them stepped in front of the pass. Interception!

There were groans from the Sexsmith crowd.

Brad got to the sideline and pulled off his helmet.

Coach Henderson came over to him. "Again, I am going to ask: what's wrong with you?"

"Nothing, Coach," Brad said, red-faced. "I will find a groove. Give me a chance."

The Sexsmith defence didn't allow the interception to hurt the Shamrocks. On two straight plays after the Prospectors got the ball, the Shamrocks linemen came pouring through the line and sacked the quarterback. After a Peace River punt that went out of bounds, Sexsmith had the ball back.

Coach Henderson made hand signals at Brad, who had the Shamrocks offensive players huddled around him on the field. The coach was calling for a running play. He didn't want his shaky starting quarterback dropping back to pass again.

Brad took the snap and attempted to hand off the ball to his left. Trouble was, the running back — as called for in the playbook — was to the right of Brad. Instead of having the ball hit the running back's hands, it fell out of Brad's hands and onto the grass.

Fumble!

Brad got down to his knees to try to cover the ball, but a Prospectors lineman dove and got to it first.

Coach Henderson grabbed his cap off his head and threw it to the ground. As Brad scampered to the sidelines, Coach Henderson dashed out to meet him.

"Brad. Sit down!" the coach yelled.

"What?" said Brad.

"I said sit down! We're going to give Gabe a try. You aren't paying attention. You're sluggish. Your head isn't in this game!"

Coach Henderson came over and tapped Warren on the shoulder, then motioned Gabe Wilkins, the team's back-up quarterback, to come over.

"Okay, Warren," said the coach. "Get some footballs and play catch with Gabe. Get him warmed up. He's going in."

The coach walked back to the spot where Brad had

taken a seat, as ordered. "And as for you, young man, I am disappointed. Something is really wrong with you today. But you won't tell me. Instead you go out there and put your teammates in a bad spot. It's not me you're letting down, it's them. You're distracted; you aren't paying attention to the game. So, Brad, for the good of the team, you have to sit."

Coach Henderson left Brad to sit by himself on a section of the bench.

After he had finished tossing the ball back and forth with Gabe, Warren took a seat next to Brad.

"Is it because you didn't sleep?" Warren asked. "Are you too exhausted to play?"

"Shh, Warren," said Brad. "I'm the team captain. I am supposed to be a leader. I can't tell the coach I can't play because I didn't sleep. That I couldn't sleep because I am worried that someone might find a photo of us cheating against the best team in the league. Wouldn't sound good, would it?"

"Guess not," said Warren. He stood and walked away just as Gabe completed his first pass of the game on the field.

13 SPEAKING HIS MIND

Brad and Warren sat on a wooden bench in the dressing room. The rest of their Shamrocks teammates had filed out, but they still had on their shoulder pads and green jerseys.

"Boys," said Coach Henderson, "it's not detention, You can get changed and go home."

Despite Brad's poor performance, Coach Henderson was smiling. Why? Because the Shamrocks had won.

With Gabe at quarterback, the offence was able to move the ball into Prospectors territory time after time, drive after drive.

Without an experienced quarterback, the team had a hard time getting into the end zone. But the week of practices had made an impression on the defensive players. Throughout the game, they chased down any Prospector who touched the ball. They sacked the quarterback and wouldn't let the receivers catch passes. And with a few field goals from Pete, the defence showed it could protect a lead. A 12–3 win didn't really entertain the Sexsmith parents and fans who came out to see the game, but it was far better than losing.

The Shamrocks could celebrate the fact that they'd won two games out of three — even if their two wins were by the skin of their teeth and their loss was a blowout.

By Monday, it was clear that the whole town was in the throes of Shamrocks fever. Warren was on his bike, heading to the restaurant. He turned onto Main Street, then slammed on his brakes. He saw a poster in the front window of the grocery store. On it was the same picture as on the sign at the Shamrocks home field —the football players silhouetted in the sun. And the poster had the same motto, "*Where the Shamrocks Grow.*"

Under the picture and the motto, the poster advertised a rally:

> *Shamrockin' Shamrally.*
> *FRIDAY NIGHT*
> *COMMUNITY CENTRE*
> *7 p.m.*
> *JOIN SEXSMITH in*
> *CONGRATULATING OUR TEAM!*

The win over the Prospectors, no matter how ugly it was, had given the Shamrocks a 2–1 record and a tie for first place at the top of the league standings. Coupled with the win over the mighty Raiders, the whole town had a reason to party.

Warren got back on his bike. He pedalled past the hair salon and saw another Shamrally poster in its window. And then he came to the front door of the Jade Garden, where he saw not one, not two, but three of the Shamrally posters in the front entrance.

From inside the restaurant, his dad saw Warren staring at the window. He pointed to the poster and then at his son, smiling widely.

Dad is actually proud of me, thought Warren.

Warren rode his bike around to the back of the restaurant, locked it up in the alley and entered, as usual, through the kitchen. He grabbed his textbooks and sat down at the family table.

There were only a few people having early dinners. It was Monday and it was just past four o'clock. The dinner rush wouldn't start for another hour.

But Warren recognized one person sitting at a table, trying to master chopsticks. She was picking up a piece of chicken, her hand shaking as the meat rolled between the two sticks.

Warren's mom came by, offering the diner a fork and knife. The girl shook her head.

"I can do this," she said.

It was Bridget. After she managed to raise the chopsticks to her lips, then gingerly rolled the chicken into her mouth, she turned and saw Warren. She put up one finger as she chewed. Warren saw her swallow her bit of food and ask her parents if she could be excused from the table.

Bridget stopped at Warren's table.

"Hey," Warren said. "This is unusual. Your family usually comes here on Wednesday."

Bridget's eyes narrowed. "Oh, you noticed that. So you're a bit of a spy, huh?"

Warren went quiet. A few weeks before, he would have been happy for Bridget to notice him. If she had just said hello to him he would have been over the moon. But now he didn't like the sly smile she gave him as she said, "I'm just messing with you."

She turned her back to the front of the restaurant — and her parents. "Warren," she whispered, her smile disappearing. "It's done. I was able to get into a computer lab today, alone. I found the file and deleted it. I looked for copies and I didn't find any. So, it's gone."

Bridget turned and walked back to her table. She sat down and picked up the chopsticks. Warren watched her reach the sticks into the bowl and try to close them on some noodles. The noodles slid like slippery snakes through the chopsticks and back into the bowl.

Bridget had just given Warren the news he'd been waiting for days to hear. But it didn't make him feel any better. The file was gone, the secret was safe. So why was that feeling in his stomach still there?

Warren got up and walked to the table where Bridget sat with her parents.

"Hello, Mr. and Mrs. Mason," he said.

"You must be Mr. Chen's son, Warren. You're the

one who scored that touchdown!" said Mrs. Mason. "Nice to meet you. You know Bridget?"

"Yeah, from school," he said. "If you'll excuse me, can I show Bridget something?"

Bridget looked at Warren, her eyebrows raised.

"You know, no one will judge you if you use a fork and knife," said Warren. "After all, this is Chinese food that, well, isn't really Chinese food. Most of this stuff was invented for people in North America, and that's what you call Chinese food here."

"I still want to learn how to do this," said Bridget.

Warren put his hands on hers and slid the chopsticks through her fingers. "Okay, then," he said. "Right between the finger and thumb. There. This will make it easier. And when you eat, hold the bowl in one hand and bring it right up to your mouth. Chinese people don't think it's rude for you to pick up your plate or bowl. Then you can use the chopsticks to move the noodles from the bowl to your mouth."

"This must come easy for you," said Bridget.

"Are you kidding?" said Warren. "I had to practice for months!"

Then the tone of Warren's voice changed. Less playful, more serious.

"Yeah, to really learn something, you've got to practice. You've got to stick with it. It doesn't matter if it's using chopsticks, or running a business like my mom and dad do, or playing football — or your homework."

Bridget's mom and dad both nodded.

"Good advice, Warren," Mrs. Mason said.

Bridget's parents didn't notice how red-faced their daughter had become, but Warren did. When he went to the table, he didn't know he was going to make that comment about the homework. But he realized he meant it.

★★★

Warren and his teammates were in the Shamrocks dressing room, slipping their green team jerseys over their street clothes. They could hear chanting and clapping from outside. It sounded like everyone in Sexsmith had come to the field for the Shamrally.

"Hey, Warren, lighten up!" said one of his teammates. "We've been looking forward to this all week! Why do you look so sad? I hear they are going to give you a special mention because of that touchdown run! They'll probably even ask you to make a speech."

That was what Warren was afraid of. As he arrived at the community centre, the coach had pulled him aside and told him he had something special planned.

"We want to show everyone in town that anyone can be a Shamrock," said Coach Henderson. "How you can contribute, even if you think you're too small. We are going to celebrate the fact that you took your chance and ran with it." He laughed at his own pun.

"Ran with it, get it?" he said, nudging Warren.

It took all of Warren's mental strength to convince his legs not to start running there and then. Not to run away from the Shamrally and find some quiet spot somewhere in town where he could hide.

Coach Henderson walked into the dressing room. "Okay, boys, line up! We have a big crowd outside and I want us to make an impressive entrance. We'll line up and run out one by one, starting with our defensive players."

The dressing room door and the door that led outside both swung wide, held open by volunteers. Warren heard the name of the first player on the defensive team announced on a loudspeaker system. Then the roar of the crowd. To Warren, it felt like the whole town was screaming in his ear — and Warren was still in the dressing room. The first player dashed through the two doors, ready to soak up the applause.

The next player was announced. And the next. With each Shamrock, it came closer to Warren's turn.

Brad stood behind him. As the team captain, he'd go last. Warren was the touchdown hero, so he was given the honour of going just before Brad. The pair knew they would get the biggest cheers of the night.

Finally it was Warren's turn. He stood at the door, waiting to run out into the cool fall evening.

"And here he is…your touchdown herrooooooooooo. Warrrrrr-en! CHEN!" cried the announcer.

"Go!" One of the volunteers patted Warren on the back. "Go now!"

But Warren's feet were pressed into the floor, as if each leg weighed a ton. Warren remembered reading in a science book that Jupiter had much stronger gravity than Earth. He felt so heavy, he could have been on Jupiter.

"Go!" the volunteer cried again.

"Warren, what's up?" Brad hissed from behind.

"I can't do this," Warren said. "Brad, I've got to tell the truth."

"Now?" cried Brad. "But this is the rally! Does it have to be here? Now?"

"WARRRENNNN CHENNNNNN!" the announcer cried again.

"Yes," sighed Warren. He knew he was going to do it. He had to tell his secret. And as soon as he committed to doing the right thing, Warren's legs started to move. They felt light as he sprinted into the evening air.

Warren didn't hear the crowd chanting his name. He didn't notice the people clapping. All he could see was the podium set up on the grass. And he knew that he was going to stand at that podium, speak into that microphone and make a very public confession. He wasn't nervous anymore. In fact, he couldn't wait to get up there, to get rid of that queasy feeling in his stomach once and for all.

14 PLAYING WITH HEART

Warren looked behind him and saw Brad, the final Shamrock running onto the field to the applause of the crowd.

After the noise died down, Coach Henderson went to the podium, adjusted the microphone and addressed the crowd.

"Thank you, ladies and gentlemen, parents, visitors," he said. "Wow. Your support of Shamrocks football is amazing."

"You're gonna go through with this, aren't you?" Brad whispered to Warren as they watched the coach speak.

"I'm sorry, Brad, but I have to," Warren whispered back.

The coach continued his talk: "Before I introduce the player who gave us our first win over the Raiders in years, I want to say something about our team. While that one player scored the winning touchdown, it was just one play in a long season. We still have many games to go. We need more wins — and the fans' support — to get us pointed toward a league title. We have had our ups, we have had our downs.

"And while we got that big touchdown against the Raiders, it required the whole effort of the team to set up that play. Last season, we lost so badly that one big play, even five big plays, wouldn't have mattered. But this year is different. Our defenders made big hits. Our kicker made some big field goals. We hung close to the team that everyone was telling us would beat us by a mile. And it set *this* boy up to make the big play. And *this* boy —"

A roar from the crowd drowned out the coach's words. He took a step back from the microphone to let the noise die down, then resumed his speech.

"This boy symbolizes everything great about the Shamrocks. There's a right way and a wrong way to play — and we play the right way. With decency."

Warren wanted the coach's speech to be over. He had some business to attend to — and he didn't want to lose his nerve. The more he had to wait, the more he'd be tempted to chicken out.

The coach made a *harumph*-ing noise into the mic and continued: "When I first saw Warren, I thought, really, he's so small. Could he really play this game? But the Shamrocks have always been about giving everyone a chance. What matters is your courage, your heart. And Warren Chen showed me he's as quick as a cat, tough as a bear. He proved how much he wanted to play. And here he is!"

The crowd roared and Coach Henderson pointed at Warren with the mic. Warren took it and climbed onto the podium. He paused, looking first at his coach, then into the crowd. He saw Bridget Mason and her family. He saw a lot of familiar faces, people he'd seen at the restaurant over the years. He saw the reporter from the *Herald-Tribune* holding a smartphone aloft, recording what was being said so she would have quotes to use in her article.

"H-h-h-hello," Warren stuttered into the mic. The coach gave him a reassuring pat on the shoulder. And then a thought crossed Warren's mind. *What if I don't say a thing? There's still time. I can still keep this secret.*

But then Warren saw his father in the crowd, sitting with his mother and sister. Looking straight at his family, he knew what he had to do. It was time to do the right thing. He had to pretend he was talking to his dad, and his dad alone. He'd confessed to his dad a bunch of times, from the time he jammed the dishwasher at the restaurant to the time he tried to sneak out after he'd been grounded.

"I want to say I'm s-s-s-s-orry," Warren began.

The crowd went quiet. Then there were whispers of confusion. Their touchdown hero was apologizing? For what?

Warren continued, eyes focused on his father. "A

few weeks ago, I was scared. Not scared of playing football. I love the game."

A cheer from the crowd interrupted Warren. He
paused for a second and something in his face made the
cheer die down.

"I was scared of not playing well enough. So I did
something wrong in that game against the Raiders. I
was tackled. I mean, I was tackled short of the goal line."

There, the worst of it was out. "But I danced like
I'd scored, and I fooled the referee. I knew it was a lie. I
knew it was cheating."

Warren touched his face. He was surprised to find
there were tears streaming down his cheeks.

"I am sorry. I guess I see the players on TV do it, and
I thought it was all right for me to do, too. I thought
if I showed off enough, we might get the touchdown
call. And we did. But I can't lie anymore. I have people
come to me on the street to talk about that touchdown
and I am lying to them by letting them believe I did it.
I tell them how I scored, when I *know* I never scored.
Please don't thank me anymore. I am not a hero."

And with that, Warren put down the microphone
and ran. He sprinted away from the field. He left his
change of clothes behind in the dressing room. He
wanted to be as far away from the party as possible.

The sick feeling in Warren's stomach was finally
gone, only to be replaced by a stinging shame in his
heart.

15 HEART TO HEART

Warren heard the front door of the restaurant open. In his mind's eye, he could see his father walk past the sign that read "*Please wait to be seated*" and toward the office where Warren was sitting.

He heard Lynn greet their father. "Warren just got here!" she yelled. "He's in the office with Mom. He's in a lot of trouble, isn't he?"

"No, Lynn, your brother is not in a lot of trouble," Warren heard his father say. "I am just glad he's back here, safe. I've been looking for him for hours."

Warren's dad opened the office door. His wife was sitting at the desk, across from their son. Warren didn't look up as the door opened.

Warren's mother got up to leave the room, and paused. She turned and spoke to Warren. "Just tell him what you told me. You'll be fine."

Then his mom continued on her path out of the office. After the soft click of the office door closing, all that could be heard was Warren's sobs, sniffles and hiccups.

"D-d-d-d-ad." Warren's voice was muffled, as his head was buried in his arms. "I am so sorry. It's just that we w-w-w-w-anted to win so b-b-b-adly, and —"

"And it was like the pros you watch on TV," said his father quietly. "But all they do is show the world how foolish they look."

"No one ever calls them cheaters."

"No, because they make lots of money. They're on TV and in magazines every day. But Warren, you need to remember that they are celebrities, which means they don't need to answer to their families or their fans, or anyone. Just because they are famous doesn't mean they are right.

"I don't know football all that well," he continued, removing his glasses and wiping the lenses with a tissue. "But I do know something about sports. It doesn't matter if it's football or soccer or field hockey. You play sports so you can learn teamwork and respect. Ninety-nine point nine per cent of the players who play as kids will never be pros. But anyone can take those lessons forward. You need teamwork in the restaurant, or if you start another business, or if you become a doctor and work at a hospital. Respect the game and you will get a lot from it."

"D-d-d-ad, I know I embarrassed you. That's why I am going to quit the team."

"Shhh." Warren's dad shook his head. "That is exactly why you *won't* quit. If you quit, you're running away from the problem. No, Warren, you'll keep playing, keep impressing your coach and keep impressing me. And you'll live down what you did. It'll be tough, but it will make you a better person. You can prove to everyone you have the strength to bounce back from this. I might be a little worried when I see you play against boys twice your size, but I am more scared of what would happen to you if you quit and took the easy way out."

Warren couldn't believe what he was hearing. He had been so sure that his dad would demand he'd quit football, he'd never thought about what would happen if he stayed. Fans would laugh at him. Referees would think of him as a cheat.

But I can do it, thought Warren. He could prove that he respected the game.

"But, Dad, what if the coach kicks me off the team?" Warren asked.

"Let me worry about that," said his father. "I've already spoken with him. We both think it's best if you stayed on. That is, after you serve a two-game suspension set by the team. And we have to wait to see if the league has any discipline for you. Warren, you're not in this alone. After you ran off, your team captain spoke to the crowd. He said he found out and also decided to keep it a secret. He said he should have told your coach. But he said you inspired the whole team with your dedication. Everyone was amazed how, despite your size, you didn't quit. While I was sad to hear about the cheating, I was proud to know how highly your teammates think of you. And then we all realized you'd run off."

Was that a smile on dad's face? Warren could have sworn that the corners of his dad's lips turned up.

"Look, son, we all have choices. And even if you don't make the right decision at first, it's what you do afterward that's important. Did you know that I made a big mistake too, once? You know that I dreamed of owning a restaurant ever since I arrived in Alberta from Hong Kong. I was working in my cousin Don's restaurant in Fairview, hoping to save up for a place of my own."

Warren had been with his family a few times to eat at Don's place, the Moon Palace. Not bad, but not as good as the food at the Jade Garden.

"Well," his father continued. "I'd only saved some of the money that I needed. And one night, at closing time, I was sweeping the floor and I found a lottery ticket. I didn't think much about it, but I didn't throw it out. When I checked the newspaper, sure enough, it was a winner! The next day, an older man and his wife — I used to see them eat at the restaurant every Sunday — came in and asked if we'd seen a lottery ticket. And you know what I did, son?"

"Gave the ticket to them?"

"No. I lied. I told them I hadn't seen it. I was going

to cash it in. It would have been more than enough money to buy and set up my own restaurant. I took down their number and pretended that I would look for the ticket. I told them I would call them if it turned up."

"But," said Warren, "if you claimed the prize, they would have said the ticket was theirs."

"It would have been their word against mine. They hadn't signed the ticket. There was nothing to prove it had been theirs. So I figured I'd give it a few weeks, then drive down to Edmonton and claim the prize."

"Then why aren't we millionaires?" asked Warren.

"Because, well, the more I thought about it, the worse I felt about it. I had been thinking about what I'd do with the money, not about what it might mean to them. What had I stolen from them with the ticket? So after a week of sleepless nights, I called them. I could have told them that I had just found the ticket, but I told them the truth. That I had found the ticket and lied to them. That I was going to take money that was rightfully theirs."

"Were they mad?"

"I thought for sure they would be." The corners of his mouth turned upward again. Warren saw it. There was no doubt about it. His dad was smiling. "But instead, they thanked me for doing the right thing. See, I made the first mistake, but I made up for it. In fact, the couple was so happy they put aside some reward money for me and . . ."

Warren took a deep breath and finished his dad's sentence, ". . . And gave you the money to open the restaurant."

"Yes," said his dad. "That was exactly what they did. Now it's your turn to do the right thing. Keep playing football. And practise. And help your team win games . . . the right way."

16 BACK IN THE GAME

Coach Henderson stood on the sidelines. The autumn days had given way to a snap of winter in the air. Any day there would be snow on the ground. Coach Henderson blew his whistle as he watched all the Shamrocks players on the field, running pass patterns, smashing into tackling dummies, doing their calisthenics.

All, that is, except for Brad and Warren. They stood beside their coach, wearing street clothes. The air was cold enough to see their breath. Warren looked at his watch. In half an hour he'd have to meet Bridget at the restaurant for her math tutoring session.

The Monday after the Shamrally, Bridget had gone to the principal to confess their scheme.

She was required to re-submit all the assignments that Warren had done for her. But the principal had told her there was nothing wrong with Warren acting as her math tutor. He couldn't write the assignments for her, but he could work with her to help her understand the math problems.

"That's teamwork, not cheating," the principal had said.

The coach blew the whistle to signal that practice was over. He called the team to form a circle around him — including Brad and Warren.

"Boys, as you know, I have suspended Warren and Brad for two weeks for their roles in covering up what happened in our first game of the season. And before practice, I talked to the league convener and Coach Klimchuk from the Raiders."

Warren was so worried about the league's decision he could barely breathe. And he hoped for the sake of the team that Brad would not get punished as severely as he would. After all, Brad's only crime was not talking.

"Brad and Warren," said Coach Henderson. "Tomorrow you both come to practice in pads."

"What?" said Brad. "We can both play?"

"Well, once the Raiders and the league got all the facts, they agreed to limit your punishment to the suspension we had already given you. They know you boys have to live this down. When they heard that you confessed in public, they felt that took a lot of guts on your part."

"What about the game?" asked Warren.

"Coach Klimchuk said he won't protest the game. In his mind, his team didn't deserve to win, anyway. He said that, since his team put themselves in a position to be beaten by one bad call, they didn't deserve to win. The league agreed."

Warren leaped into the air.

"Whoa, whoa!" said Coach Henderson. "You may be happy, Warren, but this is where the hard part begins. You see, Coach Klimchuk also said that the Raiders are looking forward to seeing us in the playoffs. They'll be gunning for us. They'll be gunning for you."

Warren didn't care. After the awful feeling of keeping a terrible secret for two weeks, trying to avoid a bunch of Raiders players didn't seem like a very hard task at all. Warren knew that he'd have to practise hard and earn back the respect of his teammates. The coach had warned him that it was likely he wouldn't get the benefit of the doubt from any referee in the league. Any close call would go against Warren.

So even more than at the start of the football season, Warren knew he had to prove to people that he could play football; that he could play it right. And he was ready.

BE A PRO!
KNOW THE LINGO

Football is a game that's popular throughout North America. But the versions of the game played in the United States and Canada are slightly different.

This guide will help readers understand the game as it is played in this book.

downs: Each play run in the game is called a "down."
In America, the offence has to gain at least 10 yards within four downs. If it does get the 10 yards, it gets a "first down," meaning it can keep the ball and try for another first down or to score a touchdown.
In Canada, the idea is the same, except the offence has only three downs, not four.
If, on fourth down (in America) or third down (in Canada), the coach decides that his team won't get the yards it needs, he can choose to either punt the ball to the other team or try a field goal.

out of bounds: To be "in bounds" in America, a receiver needs to have both feet inside the lines as he catches the ball. In Canada, the receiver only needs to have one foot in.

players on the field: In America, each team has 11 players on the field. In Canada, each team has 12 players on the field.

punt: The punter drop-kicks the ball and the opposing team has to retrieve the ball.

size of field: In America, the field, from goal line to goal line, is 100 yards long. Each end zone is 10 yards deep. In Canada, the distance from goal line to goal line is 110 yards, and the end zone is 20 yards deep.

scoring: In Canada, you can score in every way that you can score in America.

touchdown: Running with or catching the ball in the end zone, six points

conversion: After scoring a touchdown, a team can either try to kick the ball through the uprights for one point, or try to run or pass the ball into the end zone for two points.

safety: If the defence tackles an offensive player in his own end zone, the defence gets two points.

field goal: An offensive team decides to try and kick the ball through the uprights, from anywhere on the field. It is rare to see field goals longer than 50 yards. But, in Canada, you can also get rouges (see below).

rouges: If the offensive team kicks the ball into the end zone, either a missed field goal, punt or kickoff, it is worth one point.

ACKNOWLEDGEMENTS

I would like to express my gratitude to Coach Kelly Lenek and his staff at the Sexsmith Shamrocks, for allowing me to watch their drills and ensuring I had a good understanding of Bantam football in the region. Even though this is a work of fiction, I wanted the story to feel as "real" as possible, and the Shamrocks were wonderful in answering my questions and letting me see their team in action.

MORE SPORTS, MORE ACTION
www.lorimer.ca

CHECK OUT THESE OTHER SOCCER STORIES FROM LORIMER'S SPORTS STORIES SERIES:

PLAYING FOR KEEPS
by Steven Sandor

Hockey is everything in Branko's small town, which makes a star soccer keeper like him feel like an outsider. It's not until a video of a spectacular save he makes goes viral that he discovers acceptance is a two-way street.

BREAKAWAY
by Trevor Kew

When Adam's new friend Rodrigo introduces him to soccer, it isn't long until Adam discovers why it's called the beautiful game … but it'll take a whole lot more time to convince his dad to let him play.

MAKING SELECT
by Steven Barwin

Tyler has lived and breathed hockey for as far back as he can remember, and this year it seems to be paying off — he's *this close* to achieving High Performance Athlete status. But then his game starts to slide and he thinks taking a break from hockey would do him some good . . . if only his parents would let him.

LORIMER

KAYAK COMBAT
by Eric Howling

Everyone on the kayaking team knows that Cody is the best paddler. But they weren't counting on the arrival of a new teammate who can out-paddle them all. And if that wasn't bad enough, the guy's also a class-A jerk.

CAMP ALL-STAR
by Michael Coldwell

Jeff's been invited to an elite basketball camp, and he's looking forward to some serious on-court action for two weeks straight — but Chip, his completely unserious new roommate, has other plans for them.

WICKET SEASON
by Gabrielle Prendergast

In Winnipeg, Harry was a cricket star. Then he moves to Toronto and suddenly he's just one more West Indian kid who loves the game. In order for Harry to make the varsity team at his new school he'll have to prove himself to the coach — and it won't be easy.

NOT OUT
by Dirk McLean

Since his parents' death, Dexter has had trouble controlling his anger. When he snaps one day and gets kicked off the baseball team, his friend Atul suggests he try out for the school cricket squad. Despite his Caribbean heritage, Dex isn't sure it's the game for him.

LORIMER

MAN-TO-MAN
by Bill Swan

Michael O'Reilly is the shortest kid on the lacrosse team, and the youngest. He doesn't play rough, and everyone says he's not tough enough for the sport. When tension breaks out between teams and one team accuses the other of racist behavior, Michael realizes that he is tough after all — he's the only one brave enough to speak the truth.